CONFLICT IN THE CITY

CONFLICT
IN THE CITY

PHILIP M. COHEN

LUMINARE PRESS
WWW.LUMINAREPRESS.COM

Printed in the United States of America

Cover Illustration by Diane Demeter

Luminare Press
442 Charnelton St.
Eugene, OR 97401
www.luminarepress.com

LCCN: 2021916493
ISBN: 978-1-64388-086-0

To the wizards of words and sirens of song,
too numerous to count.
To Cubby, Art and Keith, my lodestones.
And to Al and Freida, Sam and Rose, Philip and Jennie.
The light still shines brightly.

CHAPTER 1

I t was another sweat-filled, beer-spraying, loud, and rau-
cous set. The club held maybe three hundred people who
had all come to see the headliner, a local band with a
decent following. The club itself was legendary—in the past
major bands from all over the world came to town just to
play on this stage. And all the local bands that eventually
achieved the dream played here too. But now in 2019 it
was just another stage, famous in name only. Bands paid
to play here.

"Here's 300 tickets," said the club booker. "Sell them for
whatever you want. Give $500 to the club. You can open
for Act 8."

Let's see, if I had 300 friends who would come out on a
Monday night I could charge them $2 a piece and we could
split a hundred bucks. Or a hundred friends and charge
them $5 each. We would play for free, but what else is new?
Hmm, not sure the price is still right. Or that I could scrape
up 100 willing souls on a Monday night. How about 50
at $2.50? Well, the reality was 15 souls willing to pay $10
each, and we scrounged together the rest of the club's cut
between the four of us.

But that doesn't matter, we claimed, because in the
end it's all about the music. The saintly, profane, semi-

religious act of strapping on a sonic instrument of prayer and performing a sacred act of pleasure and pain in front of however many sympathetic or curious or bored or "Gee, didn't the Doors play here, but man it's fallen on hard times" tourists. And it was a sacred act—or at least the most fun a guy can have without taking off his clothes.

How can I describe it without seeming simplistic? You know how you can anticipate your birthday? All your family and friends will be there, they all love you and can't wait to see you. And they're bringing you presents! Maybe that video game you've been dying to have! And there'll be drugs and booze. And maybe Mary will get drunk and crawl onto your lap like at Joey's party.

And then it all happens—at once! In a forty-minute cyclone of noise, rhythm, screaming, singing, and joy. And even Tommy Tourist thinks this is pretty cool, maybe this old dump isn't completely past its prime. All is great, any thought of having to pay the S.O.B. club owner to perform gets washed away.

All except for that fat, loudmouth drunk in front of the stage. Disheveled, slamming against people and shouting, "Act 8! Act 8! We want Act 8! Get the fuck off the stage! Act 8!"

Now I don't care while the music's playing. Loudmouth can't compete with Marshall amps. But he continues to bellow between songs. "Act 8! Bring on Act 8!"

This continues unrelentingly throughout the show. Until all I can see and think about is Loudmouth. I can't remember the words to the songs, what song is next, where we are, or what we're supposed to be doing. "Act 8! Act 8! Act 8!" I rush to the front, grab Loudmouth by the shirt, and bellow into his face, "Shut the fuck up!!!" I release my grip, and he falls back into the crowd as if shot.

Blessed silence. I count off the last song, and we finish in glory.

CHAPTER 2

Johnny Whoops slouched back in the pink plastic seats and stared at the grimy ceiling. It was old cardboard tiles, grimy gray and probably not cleaned since the club opened in '64. Johnny could imagine Jim Morrison staring up at the same tiles after a set in '67 and thinking the same thing. He took a drag on the joint that Billy passed him, flicked a lock of sweaty black hair out of his eyes, and watched as the smoke billowed toward the tiles. Not a bad place to be. Back stage at the world famous Whisky (né a Go Go), having just played before a roomful of music and film industry types or wannabe types. Not too hard to imagine this place in its prime. When the music scene was just forming in Hollywood and any kid from Kansas could roll into town and live out his dreams. At least as far as those dreams would really take him. Now that kid better load up his Instagram account if he wants anyone to pay attention to him.

"Hey, Space Mahn, whatta d'ceiling tell you now? Mr. Fah Away and Who Knows Where," Billy laughed as he took the joint out of Johnny's lips. "You been floating to that ting all night. 'Cept when Shirl come round."

"A man has to relax, brother," answered Johnny, thinking of the pixie cut black hair moving off her face as his girlfriend, Shirlee, looked up at him before the gig. He looked for her around the eight-by-six space that passed as a dressing room for the "headliner." Frank, named Francis after Black Francis by his Pixies-loving mother, was the band's teenage bass player, his long stringy brown hair matching his long skinny frame. He was holding court in one corner, sizing up the girls who always seemed to be there for him. Batter Up Beans (Roberto Benitez), the drummer, from East L.A. with an associate's degree from Pasadena City College, his head shaved bald, sat motionless, his feet out on top of a coffee table, watching his iPad as the sounds of a news report filtered out. Billy, the guitarist, was a White boy with dreads who told everyone that he grew up in Jamaica and that his father was a famous musician there, not a dentist from the San Fernando Valley. Johnny, Billy, Frank, and Beans, known to that minor part of the public who cared as Conflict, knew they hadn't reached the apex of true headliner. But that's what dreams are all about. And they were playing the Whisky. Just maybe thirty years too late.

"John! Hey Johnny! How's it goin'? I swear, it coulda been 1983 out there!" A sparkplug of a guy brushed his black curly hair off his forehead. "And the chicks! Going wild. I swear, there for the picking."

"OK. Harry, sure," Billy said. "So where's your little chickadee, huh?"

"Well, Frank, Frankie. Frank, you know what I'm talkin bout?" said Harry, eyeing the four girls surrounding Frank.

"Leave me out of this" replied Frank, twisting a strand of his long brown hair with his fingers and staring into the eyes of a mousy little brunette.

Harry, all five-foot-six, 250 pounds of him, penguined over to Johnny and plopped into the pink chair next to him.

"Really, John. You were tremendous tonight. Reeaally, really tremendous," insisted Harry, pulling Johnny toward him with a tug on Johnny's black cowboy shirt collar.

"Yeah. Thanks, Harry," said Johnny, pulling back and disentangling himself.

"Yeah, yeah," said Harry, his eyes scanning the room, distracted.

"Listen, kid," added Harry, who was all of three years older than Johnny. "Something's come up I gotta take care of. OK with you if I don't help you with the gear tonight?" Harry looked up at Johnny expectantly.

Harry had been with the guys since they started a little over two years ago. A cousin of Billy's on-again/ off-again (currently on) girlfriend Olivia, he had an old Subaru SUV, which he was glad to lend to Johnny and the boys for gigs in exchange for the opportunity to hang with the band and get into clubs for free. Plus the possibility of meeting attractive young (or not so attractive and maybe a bit older) ladies, of course. And for that possibility (and the occasional twenty bucks), he was also willing to haul amplifiers and drums into and out of the SUV, onto the stages of varying sizes—from a three-by-six-foot triangle, where only half the drums fit and the rest of the band played next to the bar, to a stage big enough for the USC marching band, with four musicians needing to create a sweeping musical maelstrom to fill the vast hall.

Johnny exhaled through his nose in derision and pushed Harry in the chest. "You're useless, you know that. What's so goddamn hot that you're gonna leave us in the lurch?" He pictured squeezing three amps and a set of drums into his beat-up blue Civic.

Philip M. Cohen

"No, no, you take the wreck. I'll get it from your place in the morning," said Harry. "I'm heading out with a couple of guys."

"Guys?" asked Johnny. "What guys? I thought you had finally gotten lucky." Harry nervously scanned the room again. "Hey, what the fuck, Harry? What's the matter?"

"Nothin', nothin'," said Harry, standing up and hovering over Johnny. "Good show tonight, kid. See ya tomorrow." Harry turned and toddled off through the dressing room door.

Johnny thought it was strange for Harry to bail on the band, but at least they had the SUV. "Hey guys, let's get out of here. I'm starving."

"Me too, baby!" exclaimed a black-haired beauty bursting into the room. She ran over and pulled Johnny out of his seat and into an embrace. "You're so sexy out there." She looked Johnny in the eyes, inches away. He pulled her head to him and they kissed. "That's what I like," she mock swooned, stepping away.

"Y'always were a teaser, Shirl," said Billy from across the room, having taken in the entrance. Midtwenties, cutoff jean shorts ending before they began, and a men's white shirt tied around her waist—all the guys in the band took in her entrance.

"And a pleaser, baby," Shirlee responded, draping her arm over Johnny's shoulder.

"All right. Frank, Beans, you ready?" asked Johnny, his left arm around Shirlee's waist. "Who's for the 101?"

"Pancakes!" squealed Frank. "Let's go." He pushed the little brunette off him.

Johnny the cowboy rocker, Shirlee the temptress, Billy the Valley Rasta, pancake lovin' Frank, and Batter Up Beans picked up their gear, jostling and muttering, heading for the exit.

"Doesn't seem right to be without Harry," Johnny said to Billy.

"Yeah, the mahn always pays," laughed Billy sarcastically, as they left the club.

"Oh hell, wait a second," said Johnny. He set down his guitar and amp next to the Subaru and ran to the front of the club. He could hear the guitar of the band on stage, a jangling, Byrds/Tom Petty sound. He brushed by the muscle-shirted, bald-headed Samoan bouncer, Tim, with a nod and headed up the side stairs to the office door. He knocked once and opened the door. "Hey Rog. We didn't get paid yet."

"Yeah, ya did," answered Rog, tall and stocky built Brit, late forties, blue blazer, white pants, wavy white hair, lifting a teenage blonde off his knee. "Harry was in here before you finished your set. Said he was collecting for the band tonight. I gave him three bills."

"Three large?!" exclaimed Johnny. "I need that money! What the hell?!"

"I don't know, Johnny. Pick your friends…" called Rog as Johnny left the office.

I hope Shirlee has some plastic or we're not eating tonight, thought Johnny.

They loaded the SUV like a jigsaw puzzle and hopped in, Johnny at the wheel, Shirlee next to him. Billy, Frank, and Beans followed behind in Johnny's Honda. Johnny confirmed that Shirlee had her Visa card, which she did by purring "Whatever you need," and slipping her hand onto his lap. Johnny hunched over the wheel, watching the traffic but still seeing the view from the stage. Pancakes sounded good, actually.

As Johnny drove off, a man on the sidewalk outside

Philip M. Cohen

the club watched them go. He punched in a number on his cell phone.

"Yeah, it's me," he said. "The kid is definitely in the band, and Brick drove off with his guy. Yeah." Pause "OK." He hung up and looked down Sunset at the receding Subaru.

CHAPTER 3

Harry looked out the darkened window of the black Cadillac Escalade SUV from the back seat and wondered exactly where they were headed. They were going west on Sunset, through Beverly Hills and heading toward West L.A.

"Heading for the beach?" he asked no one in particular. Neither of the guys in front answered. The driver, slicked down, close-cropped black hair above an aquiline nose, didn't move his head an inch, guiding the Escalade with minor movements of his hands. Next to the driver, the guy in the shotgun seat turned his dark brown eyes under a blue UCLA Bruins cap toward Harry and stared at him as if Harry was a bug on the windshield.

"You say something?" Bruins cap asked dismissively.

"The beach. Are we going to the beach?" repeated Harry, wondering whether he had swallowed his words in his throat.

"Yeah. Right," answered Bruins cap, turning back toward the front windshield, taking out a cigarette, and lighting it with a tarnished Zippo from his pocket. He blew the smoke up to the roof of the SUV, filling the cabin.

"Ka-uh," coughed Harry. "You mind cracking a window? Ka, ka." Bruins cap ignored him, and the driver moved his

Philip M. Cohen

hands just enough to slalom around the curves on West Sunset.

Not very nice, thought Harry. I don't know why Brick sent a couple of hard boys to pick me up. Brick knew him, all the way back to North Hollywood High days. He had the money that he had borrowed from Brick. At least some of it. Harry subconsciously patted the $300 he had gotten from Rog in the club. He'd make it up to Johnny and the boys. He stared out the window at the dark street and the high bushes surrounding the houses and street entrances to Bel Air. They continued to head west.

CHAPTER 4

The ocean was obsidian dark and the air was damp and cool as Harry stepped from the Escalade onto a parking lot near Will Rogers State Beach, a popular beach spot in Santa Monica. Harry could see the pier down the beach to his left, the lights of the Ferris wheel twinkling but no longer revolving at this time of night. All the weekend visitors, tourists, and locals had left. Harry was manhandled forward, Bruins cap taking him by the upper arm and leading him toward the shore.

"Hey, man! I'm going," he exclaimed. "Is that necessary? My shoes are gonna get ruined in this sand."

"Your fuckin' shoes are the least of your worries," Bruins cap growled, as he pushed Harry forward.

"Easy, Clifton," a soft baritone voice said in front of Harry, floating out of the night like spray from the ocean. "Harry and I are old friends. Aren't we, Harry?"

"That you, Brick?" Harry asked. "Can't see shit."

"Maybe get your eyes checked," cracked Clifton, standing behind Harry now, all six foot five of him under the Bruins cap looking like a regular, iron-pumping habitué of Gold's Gym.

"All right, you check it, Clifton," ordered Brick, not raising his voice. "I'll let you know if I need your commentary. Come here, Harry. Let's talk." He pulled Harry close, encircling his wide, sloping shoulders with his long skinny right arm.

Harry did know Brick. Or rather Bertrum. Bertrum Morgan Jr. High school drug dealer. Six feet tall and still thin as a rail. He was the guy everyone went to for drugs; first weed, E and coke, then through the full pharmacy, including uppers, downers, meth, and smack. Whatever you needed, Bertrum had it. Later of course, he expanded his repertoire to include bookmaking and loan sharking. But it was in high school that he began growing his cadre of friends, sycophants, and others hanging around for access to drugs and money.

One day a kid name of Kenny made fun of Bertrum's emaciated body, trying to impress a local lovely he was with. Kenny yelled at him, "Hey Beanpole," and laughed walking past. Bertrum grabbed a loose half brick from the crumbling school façade and swung it at the back of Kenny's head. Kenny wound up with a plate in his head and a speech impediment. Bertrum was expelled, which didn't affect his entrepreneurial enterprises, and acquired the name "Brick."

"Listen here, Harry. You have my money?" asked Brick, he and Harry facing the ocean, the waves tumbling in, water misting their faces.

Harry reached into his back pocket, extracting the wad of bills he had gotten from Rog at the club.

"Here ya go, Brick. All I could manage. Three hundred."

"Three hundred?! Three hundred dollars?" questioned Brick, with a voice even softer than before but filled with menace, like a rattler before striking. "Do you really think that's gonna be enough, $300 out of $3,000?" He looked over his shoulder at Clifton, who took a couple of steps forward.

"Wait a minute, hold on, hold o…. uh…." Harry's words cut off as he lurched forward on his knees onto the sand from the shove in the back from Clifton. The two men hovered over the kneeling Harry, his pants getting wet from the ocean tide.

"Harry, what am I supposed to do with you?" asked Brick.

"Gimme another week, Brick. I can…"

"Shut up, Harry, you fat fuck. You'll never get that money in a week. I gave you a month and…"

"I needed the money, man," interrupted Harry. "That game was a sure thing. The Dodgers never lose to the Padres."

"No such thing, Fat Boy. And by the way, I don't care. You show up here with all of three hundred bucks. Maybe I should let Clifton here get his workout for the night on your head." Brick nodded to his henchman, who stepped forward, towering over Harry like a redwood about to fall.

"No, no, wait a minute, man, wait a…," pleaded Harry, covering his head with upraised hands in what he knew was a futile gesture, bracing for the blow.

Clifton swung his arm back, only to be stopped when he saw Brick's upraised fingers.

"Harry," said Brick, getting down in the sand alongside him and placing his arm again on Harry's shoulders. "You know, this doesn't have to go down like this. After all, we could beat you to a pulp and you'd still owe me money you don't have and can't get." Harry wagged his head, his eyes wide in panic. "So what should we do?"

"Wha…, whatever you want, B…Brick."

"You know what, Harry? I just thought of something. You do this for me, and we're all square. What d'ya say?"

Harry nodded like an unhinged bobblehead doll.

Philip M. Cohen

CHAPTER 5

Shirlee woke to the sounds of traffic horns bleating and trucks rumbling outside, down the street on the north end of Van Nuys Boulevard in Panorama City. Formerly the site of a General Motors auto plant, it was now a vast shopping center called The Plant, active with shoppers from the time it opened early in the morning. And now was no longer early. Shirlee sat up in bed, rubbing her eyes and gazing down at Johnny, sleeping, moving his hand as he swiped a bug away in his dream.

She rose and walked toward a full-length mirror leaning against the purple painted wall in the small one bedroom apartment. Five-foot-four, 110 pounds, she loved the sight of her perfect small breasts and turned to admire her small but well-rounded ass. Good enough to eat, she thought. She pulled Johnny's prized Nirvana T-shirt from a chest of drawers by the bed, slipped it on and gazed out the small window, sliding it left to right to let some car-fume-laced air in. She could see the people walking up and down the street, heading toward or away from Van Nuys Boulevard on Blythe Street. An infamous area in the 1970s, the city council had barricaded the street back then to halt the drive-by gang activity and drug dealing. But now it was a reopened thoroughfare and home to new apartment buildings. Except for this building that still had the old two story, U-shaped structure of so many San Fernando Valley apartment complexes dating back to the '50s. And this one didn't even have a pool in the middle.

Shirlee was new to Los Angeles, only getting here from San Francisco six months ago. Growing up with a single mother in Fresno, she had been a quiet girl named Susanne Johnson with long brown hair and few friends who appreciated the type of rock music that made her feel alive. Fresno was mostly a country music town except for the kids from school who were either into Taylor Swift pop or rap. After fending off her mother's succession of boyfriends, her "uncles," she escaped to Portland, living on the streets and panhandling. But she tired of the street scene and moved to Seattle on rumors of a resurgent grunge music scene. After a year of searching for a scene other than coffee making, she realized the rumors were only that, wishful thinking, and traveled to San Francisco. But there the days of hippies and Haight were long gone, and Shirlee—renaming herself after her favorite singer, Shirley Manson of '90s pop rockers "Garbage" and dying her hair jet black—decided she didn't fit in there either, not with the high-tech workers and not with all those who serviced them. So down to L.A. she went, to what she hoped was her rock and roll heaven.

"We got anything to eat in here?" she heard Johnny say behind her. She turned and smiled crookedly to her rocker boyfriend.

"I think we can find something," she said as she sprang back into bed on top of Johnny.

Philip M. Cohen

CHAPTER 6

An hour later, Johnny was pouring coffee into two stained mugs in the small kitchen. He walked into the sitting room, just big enough for a tattered yellow cloth-covered couch and a thirty-inch television on the wall airing a rerun of "The Big Bang Theory," and handed one of the mugs to Shirlee, who was watching the show.

"I'm so glad it's Saturday," said Johnny, sitting next to Shirlee on the couch, coffee in hand. "I couldn't stand standing around that building giving the evil eye to innocent nobodies today."

"At least you have a job," complained Shirlee. "Only thing I've been offered is stripping at the Gold Room. Let's go out for breakfast."

"With what money? Harry took off last night with the gig money, and I haven't been able to get ahold of him." Johnny reached for his cell phone and redialed Harry's number. After four rings, he heard Harry's voice.

"Hey, hey, Harry here. What's your beef? Leave me a message." A long beep followed.

"Harry, you sack, call me already. I need that cash," Johnny said and disconnected. "There's some bread and yogurt in the fridge," he said to Shirlee, who nodded and headed into the kitchen. Johnny's phone rang. It was Billy's number.

"Hey, Bill, what's up?" Johnny answered the call.

"Ya seen Harry?" asked Billy. "Livie's here, and Harry was s'pose to come by 'n' drive her to work this mornin'." Olivia lived with her aunt, and Harry rented a room from his mom. But Olivia and Billy were going well right now, and she was spending most nights at his place.

"Naw. He's MIA, man. He and the money."

"Wha? Oh mahn. Well, call me if ya hear from dat piece of. When's de next gig?" Billy asked.

"Man, ask Harry. If he ever shows," the irritation in Johnny's voice obvious. "Listen, we should rehearse tomorrow anyway. Tell Frank and Beans."

"Aight. Catch ya round." Billy hung up.

"What the hell!" exclaimed Shirlee, as she rummaged through the refrigerator. "There's nothing to eat here but old yogurt. Ugghh!"

"Aren't we dramatic," said Johnny, thinking he had to get a new road manager. "Let's go for a walk."

CHAPTER 7

The band gathered for rehearsal the next afternoon in Van Nuys, not far from Johnny's apartment. From the outside it looked like a string of warehouses, one nondescript, square, single-story building after another, stretching for blocks north of Sherman Way, a main drag through the San Fernando Valley and an alternative when the freeway was too stacked with cars to handle. Nameplates on the front doors in one section of buildings read "Valley Toys," "Askarian Carpets," "Lowland Lighting," and "Sonic Street Studios." Passing through the heavy metal door into Sonic Street Studios was an office on the left, a large desk in the center, guitar cables and guitars for rent on the back wall, and autographed pictures of would-be music stars, rockers, country singers, rappers, and R & B groups on the wall ("Love ya, The Manic Panics," "Thanks for Everything, Crystal Springs," "You Da Bomb, F Fillie Frantic"). Down the hall was a series of eight rooms—some small, eight by ten; some larger, all the way up to twenty by twenty-five with full stage and lighting for the bigger groups. Every room had amplifiers and speakers, a drum set, and a public address system for singers.

Inside one eight-by-ten room stood Johnny, adjusting his silver guitar strap, his metallic blue Fender Stratocaster slung low on his hip, gunslinger/Keith Richards-style. Beans was behind the drums, lightly tapping each drum with a stick, checking the tautness and tone of the drumheads. His bald head glowed, reflecting the fluorescent tube lighting hanging over their heads. Frank stood to the side, turning the pegs on his Rickenbacker bass, eyes staring through his tangle of brown hair.

"Testin', testin'," Billy spoke into the microphone, standing next to Johnny, his voice projected through the suspended JBL speakers in the front of the room. "Soundin' right."

"All right," said Johnny. "Yuh ready?" he asked Beans and Frank.

"Oh, play 'Sunset on Sunset'," requested Shirlee, seated on the floor in front of the band next to a blond girl who had trailed behind Frank like a lost puppy when they entered the room. She must be skipping middle school today, thought Johnny.

Johnny strummed an E chord and began to sing.

"The day is dawning on Sunset; the street is coming alive/ And all those kids who wished it was theirs/ Hoped the day had never arrived..."

Beans cracked the snare and the rest of the band jumped in, Frank laying down a descending bass line, Billy holding a single sustained note veering on feedback, Shirlee grinning ear to ear and the little blonde staring with her mouth ajar.

"And daybreak is the end of day, on Sunset Boulevard/ You make a wish but life's in the way/ It's sunset on sunset, sunset on suns..."

"Hey guys!" a voice boomed at the entrance to the room, the heavy door slamming shut, a jarring offbeat banging clash with the music. "I love it! That a new one?"

Johnny opened his eyes and stared daggers. "Harry, you fuck! First you bail on us at the gig and now you interrupt? You know better, man," he said, his frustration dripping from his voice and evident in his face. Everyone stopped playing, the song disintegrating note by note by note.

"Come on, John. You know I never miss a rehearsal," replied Harry.

"Where've ya been, mahn," asked Billy, shifting his guitar to his left side. "No one's 'eard from ya since da Whisky. Livia thought ya mighta split town."

"Naw, naw, I didn't go anywhere," said Harry, pulling up his sagging brown pants over his protruding belly. "I was just laying low."

"Well, go lay low over there," said Johnny, indicating a corner of the room. "We're tryin' to get some work done here. All right? Let's try that one again. We better get this tight before the gig at Slim's next week," referencing a small club in North Hollywood that was a favorite of the band and their friends. He nodded to Frank, Billy, and Beans and started the song again.

CHAPTER 3

Two hours later, rehearsal was over. Johnny put his guitar in its case while talking quietly to Shirlee. Beans put his drumsticks into the stick bag, which overflowed with brushes, mallets, spare drum parts, and duct tape. Frank huddled with his girlfriend of the day, the little blonde, by the door, while Billy disconnected his cord from the amplifier, coiling it around his arm.

"Hey, Billy. Sounding great, man, sounding great," said Harry, enthusiastically clapping his hands and patting Billy on the back. "Those new songs are airplay ready!"

"Yeah, I don know bout dat, mahn," replied Billy, putting the cord into the black guitar case. "But it's a groove."

"Yeah, yeah," agreed Harry. "Listen, Billy. Do you have time to talk? I need to ask you something."

"Aw, not now, mahn," answered Billy. "I meetin' Livia at da pad. Later for dat."

"Sure, sure," agreed Harry. "What about tonight, around nine? I can meet you in Studio City in the big parking lot behind CVS."

"CVS?" Billy replied quizzically. It was a strange place to meet and talk, he thought. But what the hell. "Aight. See ya then."

"Good, good, see you then, Billy," Harry said, a big

relieved grin on his face. He patted Billy again on his back as Billy gathered his gear and headed to the door.

"What was that about?" asked Johnny, as they exited together, Shirlee leading the way. "And does he have our money from the gig?"

"Maybe tonight. Meetin' him in Studio City later. Why don chu come wit?"

"Yeah," said Johnny. "Maybe I will."

The band dispersed, everyone taking off in their rides, leaving Harry standing in the industrial park, watching the departing cars. He checked his watch, a basic Timex, and looked up to see a black Escalade at one end of the parking lot. The headlights of the Escalade flashed twice. Harry knew he was being summoned. He waddled across the lot to the SUV, a nervous smile on his face. He peered into the closed driver's side window. It slowly rolled down. The black-haired driver quarter turned his huge head to stare unblinking at Harry, then quarter turned back, slow and owl-like, his eyes looking straight ahead.

"Here, Harry, come here." Harry heard Brick's voice from the other side of the Escalade. He walked to the other side of the SUV, peering through the open passenger window. He could see Clifton filling the front passenger seat, his head brushing the ceiling.

"Did ya get it, Harry?" asked Brick, his voice slithering and soft. Harry stared transfixed into Brick's eyes.

"No, no, I didn't, Brick, I didn't." Harry anxiously tugged at his shirt. "But I'm meeting the kid later. I'll have it by the end of the night."

"OK, Harry. I'm depending on you. Don't let me down now. Right?" Brick's implied threat hung in the air, making Harry feel like gravity was pulling him into the center of the earth.

"R…, right, right, Brick," stammered Harry. "Tonight, tonight."

Brick nodded, the car window slid up, and the Escalade moved off, leaving Harry standing alone in the lot, sweat staining his clothes.

Inside the Escalade, Brick leaned back after telling the driver to head out. That fat prick better have the info, he thought. I can't believe I have to deal with this shit after all I've done, all I've accomplished. And all on my own. Money and power to burn. He thought of his lawyer father, with whom he hadn't spoken in years. After he had been finally expelled from North Hollywood High, Brick's self-righteous old man had told him that he'd never amount to anything. Well, now look at me — being driven around by my crew in my own first-class ride. Ha! Fuck high school and fuck that old asshole too.

CHAPTER 3

I t doesn't happen often. Not every time you pick up your instrument and start to play. Most of the time it's rudimentary. Practice that scale, combine those chords, sing the verse, the chorus. Even playing with others, like the band you worked so hard to put together, at times it's more painful than polished, more tangle than transcendent. But sometimes. Sometimes everything falls into place. Everything is where it should be, it's all right, and it's all right. There is no guitar line, chord, beat, bass, lead vocals, background vocals, lead, harmony, nothing but it all. All melding and merging into a whole, an indistinguishable and infinite moment when the stars have aligned, the world shifts, and time fades away. There are no thoughts, no dreams of the future, no regrets, no reminiscences of the past. There's only the now, the present moment that shines like a diamond. That elusive diamond.

Playing was spiritual, like a prayer. But not some routine, liturgically mandated, organized religion offering. More like what he imagined a Buddhist moment of enlightenment must be like. Or like Billy said, "the ultimate acid trip."

These thoughts floated through Johnny's mind as he and Billy drove down Laurel Canyon Boulevard, turned onto Ventura, and took the right into the parking lot behind the CVS, the Gap, and other stores and restaurants on the boulevard. The sky was clear, but the stars were hardly visible for all the lights that shone in the city. Johnny and Billy were driving in Johnny's trusty and dilapidated Honda Civic, having given Harry the keys and possession of the SUV earlier that afternoon.

"You see him?" Johnny asked Billy, searching for the Subaru that Harry should be driving.

"Yeah, mahn. That him." Billy pointed to the side window at the vehicle they knew too well, having transported them for over a year now. It was parked in the far corner of the CVS lot.

Johnny drove toward the vehicle, not noticing the black SUV parked nearby. He and Billy exited the Civic and joined Harry, who was standing by the Subaru, drinking a can of Budweiser.

"Oh, John, Johnny, I didn't expect you," Harry said nervously.

"What cha mean? Dis a secret rendezvous or sumthin?" asked Billy, a smile on his face, not taking the theatrics seriously.

"No, no. That's OK," backtracked Harry. "Er, listen Billy. Remember that old office your dad had? The one over in L.A.? Before he moved his practice to Tarzana? Do you remember where that was exactly?"

Billy looked at Harry as if he had asked directions to Atlantis. "Wha chou talking about, mahn? That was years ago. It musta been thirty years ago. I don know."

"Think, Billy, think," Harry insisted. "Was it in East Hollywood? Off the Boulevard?" Harry got more agitated and again started to sweat. He looked over his shoulder in quick, spasmodic motions.

"How the fuck should I know, man?!" Billy responded angrily, all traces of a Rasta man leaving his voice and the valley kid coming through. "I wasn't even born I told you."

"What is this?" asked Johnny. "What do you need this for?"

"I just do," exclaimed Harry. Sweat pooled on his upper lip. "Don't you remember? Didn't you tell me you visited your grandma there when you were little?" Harry's voice was reaching the upper limits of his vocal register, panic setting in.

"Man, I don't remember. Wha the fuck, Harry?!" Billy walked away, Johnny trailing behind. Harry yelled Billy's name behind them.

"Billy! Billy! Billy!" Harry's pleading voice blended with the sounds of passing traffic on Ventura Boulevard and faded as they walked away.

Johnny turned and waved to Harry as he and Billy slid into the Civic. Johnny started the engine and exited the parking lot onto the street.

"What was that?" asked Johnny.

"I don know, mahn, I don know." Billy's accent had returned but a worried expression creased his face as he gazed out the window.

CHAPTER 10

Johnny dropped Billy off in front of his apartment, in a pink two-story building in Reseda, only a few miles from the rehearsal space. Billy exited the car, pulling his guitar onto his shoulder and walked away without saying a word or looking at the Civic as Johnny steered back onto Reseda Boulevard and headed south. Harry's pleading voice echoed in Billy's mind and confused him. He was so insistent on getting that address. It didn't make any sense. Why the big deal?

Billy entered the lobby with a key through a glass door, punched the elevator button, and waited for the elevator to come down the two flights. He usually walked up the stairs to get to his second-floor apartment, but was too distracted and mechanically waited. The door to the elevator opened, and a girl in her midtwenties was standing there.

"Billy, back from playing?" she smiled, her expression changing to concern when she saw Billy's face. "What happened, baby?"

"Oh, hey, Liv," said Billy. Seeing Olivia lifted his dark thoughts. She was so fine, he thought—five-six, long blond hair, knockout body, beautiful face. If they were making a prototype of the classic Southern California girl, Olivia could be the model. "Aw, nothing. Where ya headin'?"

"Just over to the 7-Eleven for some coffee. You're out. Wanna come along?" Olivia's smile always got to Billy, even when he was mad at her. They had an always intense relationship, fiercely hot to arctic cold, which had been on and off since their days at Grant High. Right now the meter was back on the hot side.

"Yeah, sure," replied Billy. "Wait here. Lemme stash my gear first." He went up in the elevator, exited, and walked to apartment 210, laid his guitar on the worn brown convertible sofa in the living room, turned, and retraced his steps, taking the elevator down to the street. Billy took Olivia's hand, and they walked out the building's glass door, heading north on Reseda.

"Sure nothing's wrong, Billy?" Olivia asked.

Billy didn't want to burden Olivia with his thoughts but needed to clear the confusion in his own mind. He relayed the incident with Harry to Olivia as they walked, and the gloom seemed to lift. There was something about the incident with Harry that nagged at Billy's memory.

"Billy," said Olivia, as they entered the 7-Eleven and Billy poured hot coffee into two large paper cups. "Didn't you tell me one time when we were eating in K-town that your dad once had an office nearby?"

"Maybe. I mighta said dat. I don know. Maybe it's so. Jus can't say." Billy sipped his coffee. Did his dad have an office on Wilshire at one time? Billy couldn't recall. But even if he did, why was it so important to Harry that he would have a meltdown over it?

Billy and Olivia walked back to the apartment in silence only broken by the cars speeding up and then quickly braking at stoplights, the drivers impatient at the nonstop L.A. traffic. They rode the elevator up and entered their apartment. It was small but usually tidy, everything in its place, order drilled into Billy through his Boy Scout training and his father's strict discipline. His father had hardly been around when Billy was growing up, always at work; but when there, he was always fierce and stern with young Billy. "Get As"—anything less was sign of a poor effort. "Keep that hair neat; don't look like some hippie." It was no wonder that Billy went 180 degrees in the opposite direction as soon as his teenage years. Especially after meeting Johnny.

He inserted the key into the lock and swung open the apartment door, expecting the small comforts of home. But the place was not as Billy had left it. The one room and kitchen apartment looked like a hurricane had swept through. Billy's collection of vintage vinyl records were scattered on the floor; his guitar was out of its case, which lay open. The four drawers in the desk by the one window facing the alleyway were all pulled out and haphazardly piled onto the floor. The few wall hangings—an old poster from a Jane's Addiction concert, a weaving that Olivia had created when she took a class at UCLA Extension—were also on the floor, the frame of the poster cracked, glass fragments littering the thin brown carpet. The convertible couch had been opened, and the mattress lifted off the frame and tossed against the wall.

"Oh my god," cried Olivia, her hand to her mouth, eyes wide.

Billy looked into the small kitchen alcove. The plates, cups, glasses, and dining ware were scattered on the counter and floor, some broken. The drawers were pulled out, and food items from the open refrigerator were strewn across the room.

"Billy, Billy?" Olivia was on her knees in the kitchen, looking up at Billy as she picked up pieces of broken plates.

"My god," said a stunned Billy, surveying the wreckage. "Don't bother with that now. Let's call the police." He pulled his phone from his pocket and dialed 911.

"911. What's your emergency?" said a voice at the other end.

"Someone's broke in and wrecked my apartment." Billy gave the address, and the dispatcher said that officers would be there shortly.

Billy called Johnny and told him what happened.

"Are you two OK?" asked Johnny, after digesting the shock.

"Yeah, yeah, we're OK. But wha the hell, man? Who woulda done this?"

"I don't know, Billy. I don't know. I'm coming over." The phone line broke, and Billy looked at Olivia, who was now sitting on the floor crying. Billy sat next to her, draped his arm around her, and pulled her tight—two kids looking small as children. They sat and waited for the police to arrive, comforting each other.

CHAPTER 11

A knock at the door broke the stunned mood in the apartment. Billy lifted off the floor and opened the door to see two uniformed Los Angeles police officers standing there—a male six feet tall, a woman five-foot-five, both wearing aviator sunglasses beneath their twin brown hair.

"Afternoon. You call 911 about a break-in?" asked the woman. Billy noticed the man looking past him, surveying the room. Billy nodded yes.

"I'm Officer Garcia; this is Officer Rodriquez. Can we come in?" she asked, stepping past Billy, not waiting for his reply. Garcia saw Olivia on the floor. "Are you all right, Miss? Are you hurt?" Billy felt the eyes of both officers turn on him, their suspicion evident.

"Huh. No. Yeah," said Olivia, brushing off glass fragments from her jeans and standing. "Who could have done this?"

"Did you two have a fight?" asked Rodriquez.

"No!" Billy couldn't believe what he was hearing. His home had been broken into, and the place was obviously burglarized, yet he was being accused of something. "We walked to the store for twenty minutes, and when we came back the place was wrecked."

Philip M. Cohen

"Let's talk in private," insisted Rodriquez, leading Billy into the kitchen alcove and leaving Olivia with Garcia. Rodriquez took off his sunglasses and squinted into Billy's eyes. Billy could see that he was maybe thirty years old, not that much older than him, probably also grew up here in L.A., but yet they were from totally different worlds. "OK, first off what's your name?"

"Billy. William Bates."

"Do you live here?"

"Yeah."

"With the young lady?"

"Sometimes. You know, sometimes together, sometimes not."

"You're not married?"

"No, we're not married! What does that have to do with my apartment being trashed?" exclaimed Billy, his arms flying out to encompass the apartment.

"And did you have words this afternoon? An argument that got a little heated?" Rodriquez's eyes lasered deep into Billy.

"No! How many times do I have to tell you? We didn't have an argument, we didn't have a fight, we went to the fuckin' 7-Eleven, and came back to this shit show." Billy looked around Rodriquez to see Olivia gesticulating to Garcia and heard the words "What d'ya mean" from her.

"All right. You wait here," said Rodriquez, indicating the kitchen area. He walked through the living room, avoiding the debris on the floor and whispered in Garcia's ear. Garcia looked up, nodded, and together they moved toward the area by the front door and spoke quietly.

Billy nodded to Olivia, silently asking whether she was OK. Olivia shrugged her shoulders but nodded yes.

After a few minutes, Rodriquez waved Billy back into the living room, where he, Garcia, and Olivia were huddled.

"OK then," started Rodriquez. "We've taken down all your information and will file a report. This was probably some neighborhood junkies looking for some cash or anything they could pawn. If you realize anything's missing, give me a call at this number." He handed Olivia his card, and they turned to leave.

"That's it?" Billy called after them. "Ya come in here, practically accuse me of beating on my girl, and then just leave?"

"We're just doing our job, sir," Garcia said as she followed Rodriquez out the door. "Have a nice day." She closed the door behind her, leaving a stunned Billy and Olivia standing in the middle of the room.

Olivia entered the kitchen, found a broom, and began sweeping the debris into a pile, tear streaks lining her face.

"God damn it," cried Billy. He pulled the broom out of Olivia's hands and enclosed her in a tight embrace. Olivia's fresh tears soaked Billy's Kiss T-shirt. "It'll be all right, Livie; it's just stuff." There was a knock at the door. "Now what do those useless cops want?"

Billy opened the door to see Johnny and Shirlee standing there.

CHAPTER 12

Johnny, Billy, Shirlee, and Olivia spent the rest of the day cleaning the apartment, throwing away broken frames and kitchenware, vacuuming the carpet, heaving the ripped and destroyed mattress out the window into the alley. By the time they were finished, it was late at night, ten thirty, and they hadn't eaten since early in the day. Johnny suggested they go to the In-N-Out burger stand on Reseda and then back to his place for the night.

Billy kept going over what happened in his mind. He couldn't believe Rodriquez's explanation about junkies. Yeah, the neighborhood wasn't so great, but no one around there had ever told him of any problems before, and he had lived there for three years. It made no sense.

Johnny drove south on Reseda and pulled into the line of cars waiting to order their late-night burgers and fries. He asked the others what they wanted and mentally noted their orders. He saw that Olivia had a vacant look in her eyes as she quietly told him she wanted a chocolate shake and a cheeseburger; he could see, too, that Billy was equal parts angry and upset. The line moved fairly quickly, and the cars advanced toward the open window. Johnny placed the order, and after a few minutes, he took three bags and four drinks from the cashier, and pulled into an open parking space in the burger lot. They ate in silence, the only sounds coming from traffic on the street and from the radios playing in other cars parked in the asphalt-covered lot. A cacophony of rap, pop, rock, and Middle Eastern dance music mingled to create an eerie and disturbing blend.

Johnny remembered when he met Billy for the first time. They were still in high school in nearby Van Nuys. Johnny had hated phys ed, the exercising, the rope climbing, the running track. But he never minded the team sports that they played every few days. Whether it was basketball, volleyball, touch football, or softball, the team activities appealed to Johnny. It was similar to playing music in a band, everyone working together for the same goal. Johnny had been playing guitar for a couple of years by that time and had formed his first musical group—kids he grew up with who played '90s songs not very well.

That day it was softball for the class. The boys were divided into two groups by Mr. Dirkens, the obese and balding gym teacher, and then left to pick their positions and the batting order on their own. Johnny had noticed this long-haired blond kid who looked too skinny to hit the ball out of the infield. One of the boys, Stan, who was a year older and bigger than the others, had taken the lead in assigning positions, telling Johnny to catch and telling the blond guy to play right field, which was always where the least able person was positioned. Johnny jogged behind the plate when he heard a nasal voice with a strange accent say, "Naw outfield. Me gonna pitch."

Stan said, "What? You can't pitch. Go play out there," pointing to the vacant space in the outfield.

"Naw, me pitch," said the blond kid, not moving out of the infield.

"Get out of here," said Stan, angered that his meager authority was being questioned.

"Me pitch." The blond kid took the ball and walked to the mound. He windmilled his arm and threw a strike to Johnny.

Stan was infuriated. He walked to the pitcher's mound, pulled the glove off the blond kid's hand and threw it at his head. The kid ducked, and the glove flew through the strands of his hair. Stan ran at the blond kid and just before he reached him, Johnny jumped on Stan's back, plowing him into the ground. A melee ensued, kids piling on, standing over them shouting—"Fight, fight," "Get him, Johnny," "Kick his ass"—until Mr. Dirkens ran over and separated Johnny from Stan. After a few minutes of cooling off, Mr. Dirkens told them he didn't want to bother reporting such a stupid incident to the principal and if Johnny and Stan shook hands, he'd let it go. Johnny reached his hand out. Stan looked at the blond kid, looked at Johnny, shook his head in disgust and disbelief, then shook Johnny's hand without looking at him and ran off to play right field.

That was Johnny's introduction to Billy, who pitched the entire game but couldn't hit a lick. After the game, Johnny and Billy packed up the game gear together. They quickly discovered they both were seniors in school, both only children and, more importantly, both guitarists. They eagerly agreed to jam later that week. Johnny told his band he was moving on, and he and Billy had been close friends and bandmates ever since.

Now the two friends stood in front of the car, their burgers and fries eaten, sipping on their pink lemonades. Johnny could see that Billy was still shaken from the break-in, his pale face beneath the blond dreadlocks pinched and tight.

Billy and Olivia had told Johnny and Shirlee what they had found after returning from the 7-Eleven and about their encounter with the two cops.

"It's probably nothing," Johnny said. "Just a random occurrence. You know, this is L.A. All kinds of nonsense goes down here."

"Yeah, ja know, mahn," Billy's Rasta accent resurfacing after the effects of the trauma ebbed. "But why'd anyone pick me place, huh? Ja don have nothing 'cept me guitar and amp and some old clothes. And they din't touch de amp." Billy had a vintage Fender Reverb that he had found years ago at a pawn shop on Western Avenue in East Hollywood. It, along with his Fender Telecaster guitar, were his only prized and valuable possessions.

"I don't know, Billy," said Johnny, pausing to take a sip. "If it was junkies like the cops said, why didn't they cart away your amp? It's worth some decent money, enough for a week of fixes." He paused, looking down the street at the cars leaving the burger stand. "Listen," he finally said. "Forget about it. Why don't you and Olivia stay at my place tonight? You can have the bedroom, and we'll sleep in the living room."

"Naw, tanks but I'll feel better at my place. Back to normal and all." Billy tossed his half-full drink into the trash can. "Y'know," he said to Johnny as they and the girls climbed back into Johnny's Civic for the drive back. "It's been a weird day. First Harry going on about me old man's old address. And then this break-in. Weird."

"Like I said, man," said Johnny, wheeling the car onto the boulevard. "Random."

"Yeah. Guess so," said Billy. Olivia curled up next to him, and he felt warm and comforted. He blinked away tears and stared out the window at the passing cars and buildings.

A short drive later Johnny pulled in front of Billy's apartment building. Olivia opened the car door to get out. Johnny reminded Billy of their upcoming gig at Slim's and told him to call at any hour if he needed anything. Shirlee kissed Billy on the check and embraced Olivia. Johnny clasped hands with Billy.

"Thanks, bro mahn," said Billy. Johnny thought he had never seen his friend look so tired, so beaten down.

"Get some rest guys," Johnny said. He waved good bye as he pulled back onto the street and headed home.

"That was so harsh," said Shirlee, checking her phone for emails. "Ugh. I hate these spam mails!"

"Yeah," replied Johnny. It had been a strange day.

CHAPTER 13

Brick told the Escalade driver, Manny, to pull up to a small convenience store on Glenoaks Boulevard in Burbank.

Clifton entered the store, saw the disposable phones behind the counter among the high-end liquor, and bought one from the Armenian clerk. He also bought a scratch-off lottery ticket. Who knows, he thought. Miracles happen.

Clifton handed the phone in the packaging to Brick, who tore it open. "Pull around the block," he instructed Manny. They swung onto a dark street lined with two-story apartment buildings and the occasional lone single-story home, left over from the original construction on the street.

"Keep the engine running," said Brick. He exited the car, walked down the street to a deserted area away from the late-night dog walkers, and dialed a number.

"Talk to me," a gravelly voiced man answered on the other end. "Do you have it?"

"No, no sir," replied Brick. "I haven't heard back from that walking trash bag yet."

"And the apartment?" asked the gravelly voice.

"Nothing," answered Brick. "The kid lives hand to mouth. There was nothing there about his father except an old photo of a couple standing on a beach holding a little

40   *Philip M. Cohen*

blond baby. Figured that was the guy. But nothing about his old workplace."

"Listen, Brick," intoned the gravelly voice. "I need that address. That was the deal. Unless you can pay me that fifty large? Understand?"

"Yes sir. I got it." Brick wished he had never offloaded those Super Bowl bets. Now he was in over his head with the biggest player in Los Angeles. He knew his two guys were nothing compared to this guy's small army.

"Brace that other guy again and impress upon him you mean business. Otherwise I'll have to come up with alternatives. You're wasting my time."

"Yes sir. Got it." Brick understood all too clearly the not so implied threat. The phone line went dead. Brick looked at the phone as if a dead fish was lying in his hand. "Asshole," he grumbled to himself, ducking into the back seat of the Cadillac.

"What's that?" asked Clifton.

"Nothin'. If I was talkin' to you, you'd know. Manny, let's pay that fat boy a visit." Brick sat back and ruefully contemplated the possibilities of getting the information versus a life on the run in Mexico. His life was in Los Angeles. That fat boy had better come up with it. Brick's Spanish didn't go beyond taco and burrito.

CHAPTER 14

Harry was sleeping in his bedroom in the back of his mother's house when he was startled awake by hard, rapid knocks on the back door. He rubbed his eyes and peered out the side window.

"Shit," he muttered, seeing Brick on the other side of the door. If Brick was there, the other two goons were with him. Harry rubbed his face. This is a waking nightmare, he thought. He hurriedly wrapped a gray wool bathrobe around himself and called through the door.

"Yeah. Who is it?"

"Open up, Harry," came Brick's voice from the other side. "We gotta talk."

"Now? It's two in the morning. You're gonna wake my mom. She's sixty years old, for god's sake." Harry knew this wasn't any friendly social call.

"Harry, open the damn door, or I'll sure as hell smash it open," threatened Brick. "Clifton, get that tire iron from the car."

"OK, OK. Hold on a second. Jesus, Brick." Harry unlocked and opened the door. Brick and Clifton walked in past Harry without saying a word, Manny retreating to the car.

"Harry, you know why I'm here," said Brick, looking

Philip M. Cohen

around at the little bedroom with old chess club trophies on the shelf of a worn, plywood bookcase. The house was on a quiet tree-lined street full of fine homes in Studio City. Brick figured this pathetic guy had probably lived here his whole life, holed up in his little bedroom, never venturing far from his mother. He paced the room. "Did you get that information I need?" he asked, fingering one of the trophies.

"I tried, Brick, really, I tried. The kid didn't know anything. He must've been too young." Harry's eyes flitted back and forth from Brick to Clifton and back.

"That's really too bad, Harry," Brick said calmly.

Before Harry realized what was happening, Brick lifted the trophy and swung in a swift arc, smashing it against the side of Harry's head. Harry flew sideways, knocking over the side table next to the bed and landed on his side.

"You fat piece of shit," Brick bent and whispered in Harry's ear as he laid on the floor. "You owe me money which you can't pay. I ask you for some simple information from one of your boys, but you can't get that. What am I supposed to do?"

Harry heard Brick through the haze and the throbbing pain in the side of his head. He dimly saw Brick nodding to Clifton, who pulled Harry up by the front of the bathrobe and slapped him hard across the face. Harry tried to clear his head and scrambled toward the bed to get away, but Clifton locked his hand on his right leg, yanked him back, and kicked him in the side. Harry rolled over, gasping for breath.

Clifton reached down, picked Harry up again, and punched him in the face, Harry's nose cracking and blood erupting. Harry collapsed backwards and banged into the side table lying on the floor. Through the pain and haze of blood, he saw his old Swiss army knife in the corner of the drawer lying next to him on the floor.

"Now Harry," he heard Brick say behind him. "You better get that information by tomorrow or we're coming back to finish this fuckin j…"

Harry spasmodically swung his arm and plunged the knife into the figure nearest to him. His face raw and robe thrown open, Harry lay on the floor on his back, the knife gripped in his hand, blood dripping onto his hand. The knife had struck Brick in the right shoulder and staggered him backwards against the wall, a look of amazement and pain on Brick's face. Clifton instinctively reached inside his jacket, pulled his .45 from his shoulder holster and shot Harry in the chest. Harry's eyes widened, and he grabbed the hole in his right breast spouting blood. He closed his eyes.

"No!" screamed Brick. "Wha' the fuck?! You killed him, you asshole. Jesus."

"It was him or us," said Clifton, holstering his gun. "Come on, let's get out of here."

"Harry? Did you hear that noise? Harry?" They could hear the sounds of a frail female voice calling from the other side of the house. Clifton lifted Brick off the floor, Brick holding his hand against the knife wound in his shoulder to stanch the blood flow. He pulled Brick out the door and lifted him into the Escalade.

"What the hell?!" yelled Manny, seeing the blood on Brick's shirt. He had been half out of the car after hearing the gunshot and had to scramble back behind the wheel.

"Just drive. Get us out of here," commanded Clifton. He ripped Brick's shirt and pressed it against the wound.

"Leave me alone," complained Brick. "You asshole. Now how are we gonna get that address?"

"We'll get it," said Clifton. "We'll get it."

The Escalade zoomed down Laurel Canyon Boulevard into the canyon.

CHAPTER 15

I t was a recurring dream. I was standing alone, wearing bell-bottom jeans, purple boots, a paper hat and a red vest made of ostrich feathers. A whistling sound echoed through the sky as I looked over a deep canyon filled with water. An ancient ship, something out of a pirate movie, floated past, and a parrot circled overhead. A surfboard was lying next to me. I picked it up, launched it onto the water, and dove on top of it.

The water below the board gave way under me and dove straight down, a steep vertical fall that was never ending. I hung on desperately, fear and wonder mixing in my mind. I was terrified that this was the end of me, that the water would swallow me whole, yet amazed at the speed of the fall and the columns of water rushing past me.

Next thing I knew I was standing on the pirate ship. My paper hat was gone, and a scarf was wrapped around my head. I felt a sharp jab in my back. I turned and saw a ship full of pirates of all shapes, sizes, and sexes—men, women, boys and girls, as small as three feet and round as a bowling ball and as tall as ten feet and thinner than the thinnest willow tree. I could tell they were yelling, screaming at me, but I couldn't hear any of them. Just that eerie whistling in the air. Directly behind me was a black-haired woman dressed like Cinderella's fairy godmother, white flowing lace, a white lace crown on her head with a veil that was halfway over her face. In her hand was a sword, sharpened to a fine edge. A single drop of blood dripped from the tip, but it wasn't red. It was green. I reached behind me and felt where the sword had pricked me. My skin was hard, like bark on a tree. Tendrils were growing out of my arms, and my feet sprouted roots, and the roots sunk into the earth beneath me.

I was deep in the forest, far from any humans and abandoned by all my animal friends. I wondered what I had done to be so alone.

CHAPTER 16

Johnny sat on the bed in his apartment, strumming his unplugged guitar, the soft sounds of the chords and notes quiet enough not to disturb Shirlee, sleeping beside him. It was early morning, almost eight, and he had been up for a few hours already, unable to sleep. Thoughts of Billy and his ransacked apartment had unsettled him. Maybe he had gotten some sleep. But after a while he had gotten up, smoked a joint, blowing the smoke out the window, and began to write a new song.

Johnny strummed an E minor chord. He didn't have any lyrics beyond the title — "By Myself with You."

"That sounds good, baby." Shirlee's sleep-drenched voice rose from the bed. Johnny turned and smiled down at her.

"Yeah, just something I'm workin' on," he said.

Johnny's phone rang, playing the first few notes from REM's "Losing My Religion." He saw from the phone number that it was Olivia calling.

"Hi Livie," Johnny said into the phone. "Aren't you up early."

"Johnny, Johnny, it's Harry! Oh my god!" Olivia was distraught, her voice gasping as she talked. Johnny sat upright, putting the guitar on the bed. Shirlee was fully awake now.

"What? What is it?" she asked. Johnny put a hand up.

"Livie, what is it? What happened to Harry?" Johnny asked.

"He's—he's in the hospital," said Olivia. "St. Joe's. My aunt, you know, his mom Lori, she found him, unconscious in his room. He was shot."

"What?!" Johnny jumped off the bed. No, Johnny thought. This can't be happening. "Is he all right? Are you and Billy there?"

"What? What?" pleaded Shirlee, pulling at Johnny's T-shirt.

"I don't know. He's alive, but he's in surgery now. I don't know." Olivia began to cry.

"Johnny?" Billy's voice came through the phone. "It's me, man. We're at the hospital in Burbank. We're waiting with Livie's aunt in the waiting room."

"What do the docs say?" Johnny pulled his pants on as he cradled the phone to his neck. "Get dressed, it's Harry," he told Shirlee, who quickly shrugged off her long Van Halen T-shirt used for sleeping and dressed in her pants and T-shirt from last night that were laying on the floor.

"That he's been shot in the chest. And they'll let us know his condition when they can," said Billy. "We gotta go, man."

"We'll see you in a few," Johnny said, but the phone line was dead.

They dressed in a rush, grabbing clothes, phones, and keys, and bolted out the door. Traffic was Sunday morning light, a small favor of the gods, thought Johnny. He pressed down on the accelerator and sped along Van Nuys Boulevard. He swerved around cars waiting for the light to change and made a left onto the Ventura Freeway heading east toward Glendale and Burbank.

CHAPTER 17

Johnny maneuvered the Civic off the freeway, turned left from the off-ramp, and made a quick right into the street leading to the emergency room entrance of St. Joseph's Hospital, a six-story structure with a giant crucifix fixed to an outer wall. Johnny swung the Civic around the entry circle, grabbed a ticket, and pulled into the closest open spot. He and Shirlee ran into the hospital, scanning the room for their friends.

"Oh, Shirlee," they heard Olivia's voice calling before they saw her. Her face was reddened and streaked from tears. She ran to them and clung to Shirlee, the tears flowing down her face and onto Shirlee's check. "Who could've done this to Harry? He wouldn't hurt a fly."

"How is he?" Johnny asked Billy as he joined them standing in front of the reception desk. Billy shook his head and shrugged.

"Too soon to know," Billy said. "Come over here. Let's sit down." He motioned them to seats in the corner under the TV, which was airing the local news. They sat beside a frail-looking woman who was also quietly crying. She was introduced to Johnny and Shirlee as Lori, Harry's mother, Olivia's aunt.

They sat for an hour, talking, consoling one another,

glancing up at the clock every few minutes, and looking up expectantly every time a doctor came into the room, only to be disappointed when the doctor went to another waiting person. Johnny realized that, even though it was a Sunday morning, the yellow-walled, antiseptic-smelling room was full of people, either waiting to hear about their loved ones, family or friends, or waiting to be attended to themselves. Coughs rang out regularly, and quiet moans floated through the room every few minutes. Two uniformed LAPD officers were also in the room, talking to the hospital staff.

"Let's get some coffee, Billy," said Johnny, standing and stretching his arms to the ceiling. "Let's find the cafeteria. We'll bring you back some," he told the three women, all huddled together and quietly talking.

"What happened?" Johnny asked as they waited for the elevator that would take them down to the cafeteria.

"Livie got a call at around three this morning from her aunt," Billy started. "At first she couldn't understand what she was saying, with all the crying and sobbing. But finally she understood that Harry had been shot. Lori had heard a loud, sharp noise like a firecracker, went to Harry's room to ask him if he heard it, and found him lying unconscious, leaking blood all over the place. She called 911. The ambulance came, along with a squad car from LAPD. They patched Harry up as best as they could, attached an IV, and rushed off to the hospital."

Johnny asked if Lori had seen anyone running off. The elevator doors opened and they stepped in. Johnny pushed the basement/cafeteria button.

"No, all she said was she heard a car speeding down the street just as she got to the bedroom. Can you believe this?

First my place gets broken into and now this? Wha the hell, man?! Who'd we piss off?"

Johnny was wondering the same thing. "Do you think there's some relation between the two events? You know, Harry was awfully anxious to get that address of your dad's."

"Maybe. I don't know." Billy rubbed his head, his blond dreads swinging over his neck. "But that's ancient history. My dad retired over ten years now. And been dead for three. Plus he had his last office my whole life. At least for twenty-five years. What's so important about some office from thirty years ago?"

Johnny didn't know. He felt like he was throwing spitballs against the wall and seeing which ones would stick.

"Maybe we should cancel the gig this week," he suggested. "Big Eddie won't mind. We've been a good draw for him." The club owner always liked to see Conflict playing at his club, drawing a large, drinking crowd to the small venue.

"No, we should play," said Billy as they poured out five coffees and placed them into two cardboard trays. "We gotta play."

"OK," said Johnny. They carried the coffees up to the waiting room. A female uniformed Los Angeles Police Department officer was talking to Lori. She looked up at Johnny and Billy as they handed the coffees to Shirlee, Olivia and Lori.

"I'm Officer Shields. Who are you guys?" she asked.

"She came to the house," said Lori, indicating Officer Shields.

Billy explained their relationship to Lori and Harry, that he was Olivia's boyfriend and that Johnny was his friend.

"So he's your boyfriend?" Shields asked Olivia. She nodded her answer. Shields asked Johnny and Billy what they knew about the shooting. After speaking with them for a few minutes, she handed Lori her card. "Call me if you can think of anything else. Detectives may be coming to speak with you soon. I'm sorry about your son." Shields joined a male officer and left the hospital.

A male doctor entered the room and walked toward them. "I'm Dr. Kushogi," said the doctor, addressing Lori. He was dark-skinned, black-haired under the surgical garb. "Your son is in intensive care. We removed the bullet, but he's been badly injured. The next forty-eight hours are critical."

"Thank you, doctor," said Olivia. The doctor turned to her, smiled wanly, and walked away.

"Come on, guys," said Johnny. "Let's go. There's nothing we can do here. We'll come back later."

"You go, John," said Olivia. "I'll stay here with Lori."

"Me too," said Billy. "I'll catch up with you later."

"OK," said Johnny. He and Shirlee exited the waiting room. He wondered what exactly was going on. He and Billy often talked of their childhood—how Billy's dad had been so consumed with work and the only attention he paid Billy was that of a strict martinet, as if Billy was a plebe in a military academy. But Johnny never really knew him except as a quiet but scowling figure standing in the hall as he and Billy banged away on their guitars in Billy's room. And Harry was always the good-natured, enthusiastic friend and supporter of Billy and Johnny both. Everyone loved the guy. What could've happened?

CHAPTER 13

The next few days ebbed and flowed oh so slowly, like dripping cold molasses into a bowl of lukewarm oatmeal. Gradually Johnny and Shirlee became accustomed to the idea of Harry not being there for them all the time. Shirlee always loved how Harry would bring her little gifts—paper flowers, Matchbox cars, yo-yos, commemorative buttons he found at thrift stores. It was always a wonder to see what he'd show up with. Johnny, of course, whether he liked to admit it or not, knew he needed Harry's help in the organization, transportation, care, and feeding of the band. And these days without him brought Harry's worth to them into sharp focus. Harry might have been Olivia's cousin, but he was Johnny's and Shirlee's family too.

Olivia commuted back and forth from Billy's apartment to the hospital for three days. Lori slept there, the hospital staff providing her a room near her son.

On the third day Dr. Kushogi gave the bad news to Lori and Olivia. Harry had succumbed to his injuries and had died.

A funeral was planned at Forest Lawn in Glendale later that week. Olivia stayed with Lori at her house, though the echoes and mementos of Harry's life reverberated from wall to wall.

But before the funeral there was still a gig to play. Johnny again suggested that they cancel it, but Olivia insisted that Harry would want them to play. Those were the times Harry loved best, she insisted. And Olivia had her own personal reasons. Music had always been a crucial part of her life, from her almost-twenty years of intense listening to L.A. alternative rock station KROQ to her few years of fledgling piano lessons and now her emotional involvement with Billy and the band.

To Billy, it all felt too strange and surreal. He knew something was happening beyond his understanding and that he was somehow involved in all these horrible events, but he had no idea how or in what way. A final rehearsal for the gig was dreary and somber, everyone in obvious shock over what had happened.

The show was scheduled the night before Harry's funeral. Shirlee sent out a special invitation to their list of friends and fans stating "Special Show! Conflict in Memoriam to Harry Feldon. Forever in Our Hearts. Please Join Us…" with the date and location at the bottom.

The night of the gig Johnny drove Harry's Subaru SUV, loaded with their drums, amps, guitars, and gear toward the club in North Hollywood. Johnny was usually comfortable driving the SUV, having been behind the wheel countless times. But tonight was different. The ghost of Harry seemed to hover over Johnny's shoulder as he drove across the floor of the San Fernando Valley and down Lankershim Boulevard. Shirlee sat next to him in the passenger seat, and Billy was wedged in the back between the equipment.

They had been mostly quiet as he drove, mulling over Harry's death, thoughts of mortality, the coincidence of the break-in at Billy's apartment, and the overall sadness of mourning a friend's passing. As they drove down the street, Shirlee saw people lined up on the sidewalk.

"Must be a new restaurant," said Shirlee, indicating the crowd and knowing that Slim's was on the outskirts of Noho, the up-and-coming hip area in North Hollywood.

"No, baby, look," said Johnny. He pointed past the windshield up the street, the line stretching a block and a half, right up to the door of the club.

"Ja mahn," said Billy. "They be givin' da love for Harry bro."

Johnny pulled the SUV around the block, up an alley, and parked diagonally in a space behind the back door of the club. Frank and Beans were waiting for them, leaning against the wall.

"Hey guys," said Johnny, exiting the Subaru. He and Billy exchanged clasped hands and hugs with the other two guys. Without any of their knowledge and without any communication, all four of the band members had worn black shirts (Johnny's was a western shirt, the others all in tees) and black jeans.

"Man, it's like we got uniforms" observed Frank.

"Yeah, suppose so," said Johnny. He opened the back door of the club, entering the darkened room at the side near the edge of the ten-by-ten dance floor covered in fake wood. In front of the dance floor was a small stage, elevated by a single foot, barely big enough to fit the four band members.

"How bout some lights in 'ere?" called Billy to no one in particular.

"Hold on. One minute," came a male voice from the front of the club. The stage lights lit up, brightening the dance floor and back area. "That enough?"

"Yeah, Eddie," said Johnny, addressing the owner of the club. "That's good."

The four guys and Shirlee unloaded the SUV, and the guys assembled the equipment on the stage, plugging amps into the large speakers owned by the club, Beans attaching his cymbals to the rickety old cymbal stands of the house drum kit.

Eddie opened the front door, and the line of people snaked into the club for the bargain price of five dollars a head. Eddie didn't mind the low cover charge. He more than made up for it at the bar, selling watered-down alcohol and overpriced beer. Behind the bar was Serge, a gray goatee on his chin and a hoop ring dangling from his ear. All he needed was an eye patch, and his pirate costume would've been complete. Serge poured drinks and rang up charges as fast as he could. Tonight they could've used a second bartender.

Johnny and Billy spent the next half hour arranging pedals, checking the tuning of their guitars, and testing the level of the microphones. Beans sipped a beer in a dark corner by himself, and Frank talked to a tall redheaded girl. Shirlee circulated through the crowd, a vodka and soda in her hand. She always liked to heighten her beauty in a dramatic fashion, and tonight was dramatic for everyone. She had darkened the still-evident circles and lines under her eyes, making her black eyes shine through with a startling, nervous intensity. Not sleeping for three days had a sideways effect on her. There was something she thought of that she had to talk to Johnny about. Except right now she wasn't sure what that was.

"Oh! Hi, darling! How are you?" said a kid barely out of his teens wearing a porkpie hat, purple pants, and suspenders. "Oh my gawd. It's awful. Poor Harry. Was it a junkie? Was it a serial killer? You must be devastated!" He held Shirlee by the upper arms, squeezing her, and shaking his head.

"Yeah. Yeah, Charles," said Shirlee. She rotated her neck as far as she could without being an owl, hearing a pop on the left side. She disentangled from Charles. "It's been a bear. A real picnic." She finished her drink, reached over, and placed the empty glass on the bar.

Serge placed a stein of beer in front of a middle-aged man, short black hair, wearing a black leather jacket, all buckles and belts.

"Shirlee, girl," Serge called out. "You OK?" He was always behind the bar whenever Conflict played Slim's. He was actually always behind the bar every night. But Conflict was one of his favorite acts, and he knew the band members and their girlfriends and close friends well. They had played at Slim's at least seven or eight times, he recalled.

"Yeah. No. I'm good. I'm good," said Shirlee. "No, I, er, I'm, er, anxious to hear the band."

"Me too," said Charles, grabbing Shirlee's arm again.

"Leave it!" snapped Shirlee. She thrust her left arm upwards, knocking Charles' grip off. Her other arm pistoned into Charles' chest, shoving him backward. Charles staggered, stumbling back a few feet.

"Hey," cried Charles, embarrassed and hurt.

"Shirlee—aw, eas' girl," Serge called, his Slavic accent collapsing the three words into two syllables. "Ya gonna hurt the fella."

"Sorry, man, sorry." Shirlee patted Charles on the chest. "It's been a rough few days." She looked toward the door. There were three men inside the entranceway who didn't fit into the crowd. Older, executive-types, but not dressed like those from the record or music publishing companies, talent and management agencies who usually came out to music clubs. One was as large across as anyone Shirlee had ever seen, with a sharp, long nose. Next to him was a tall guy hidden underneath a Bruins baseball cap. Following close behind those two was a tall skinny guy, flexing his left shoulder every few minutes.

"Shirl. Hey, Shirl." Billy's voice startled her, and she turned her head toward his voice. Billy took her hand.

"Come on. Johnny be askin' for ya." He led her through the crowd, alternately pushing through the mass of people and nodding at those who let them cut through.

"Shirlee, Billy. Over here." Johnny motioned them to the side of the stage. "You too, Beans, Frank." Johnny looked intently in the eyes of each person. He knew Olivia wanted to be here too, but she was with Lori back at her house; it being too soon to leave Harry's mother alone.

"You know tonight's in memory of Harry," Johnny began. "He was the best road manager, our best friend whenever things would go wrong, and the greatest fan and supporter this band ever had."

"To Harry!" yelled Billy.

"To Harry!" the tight group of friends shouted. The shout stunned and silenced the crowd in the small club. Nobody said a word for one heartbeat…two…until someone shouted, "To Harry!"

Another "To Harry!" Then everyone yelled out, together and apart, "To Harry!" "To Harry!"

The band climbed onto the stage. Johnny counted off "One, two, three…" A crack of Beans' snare drum, and they were into it. Johnny hammered down, striking a power chord on the strings of his guitar like a shock to the senses. He sang into the mic.

"How long, howww long, how many, how long, how many, how long"

"Come along, a long, come on, come on, come on, come on"

Billy joined in.

"See if you ever, if we ever, get out of here/ See you ever, if we ever, get out of here/ Alive."

Johnny turned his back to the crowd, which had pushed up, moshed to the lip of the stage. Billy played a stinging, slow guitar solo that contrasted perfectly against the rapidly pulsing rhythm behind him laid down by Frank, Johnny, and Beans.

At the side of the stage, Shirlee swayed to the music, her mascara smudged and running down her cheeks, a mask of equal parts joy and sadness.

"Out of here-re-re-re…." Billy and Johnny held the last harmonized notes, and Beans crashed the song to a close. The crowd erupted in a geyser of cheers.

CHAPTER 13

Johnny curled the guitar cable around his arm and placed it inside his guitar case. Billy sat at the bar in the front of the club, nursing a PBR, while Frank and Beans unplugged and unattached, reversing their actions from hours before.

"Great set, Johnny," said Shirlee, draping her arm around his waist.

"Yeah, pretty good," said Johnny, wishing Harry had been there to hear it.

"Maybe he was here," said Shirlee, seeing the wistful look in her man's eyes.

Johnny opened the back door into the parking lot. Billy was talking to some tall, skinny guy.

"Who's that?" Johnny asked Shirlee.

"Him? I saw him before," said Shirlee. "He was in the club with a couple of other weird looking guys."

Johnny opened the SUV door, waiting for Beans and Frank to put their gear in and placed his guitar in a secure spot where it wouldn't be jostled as the car drove through the pockmarked, rutted streets of the valley. Billy appeared from behind, swinging his guitar inside.

"Good set, man," said Johnny. "You never played better."

"Inspired, aight?" said Billy, a lopsided grin on his face.

"I saw you talkin to some guy before. Never seen him around. He a friend of yours?"

"Mean dat dude in da parkin' lot? I didn't know him, but he say he wid a record company and wanna meet and talk bout some deal. Can you believe it?"

"I didn't think record companies were signing anyone unless they had a hit out of their bedroom and a million Instagram followers."

"Don know." Billy pulled the passenger door open and climbed into the SUV, a lit joint dangling from his lips. "But he say he wans to get together tomorra after the funeral. I got his numba." He waved a little piece of paper in the air.

Frank and Beans climbed in after Shirlee, having both Ubered to the club. The doors clanked shut, making the vehicle tight fitting and uncomfortable. But each passenger had a seat, although they were mostly on top of amplifiers.

"Yeah," said Shirlee. "The funeral." The upbeat mood of seconds ago downshifted rapidly as thoughts of Harry's end pushed all good feelings generated by the celebratory night out of their minds.

Johnny drove north on the boulevard in silence. It was late, nearly one in the morning and not much traffic on the street. Johnny looked in the rearview mirror, sneaking glances at Shirlee and the boys cramped in the back of the SUV. He was worried about Shirlee. Serge had told him of her little dust-up with Charles. He was a harmless character who often came to their shows, and Shirlee always playfully tolerated and accepted his melodramatic behavior. But tonight he had gotten under Shirlee's skin.

The effects of Harry's death were weighing heavily on everyone. Johnny felt it too. But he knew that as much as they had to process Harry's death, go through the painful emotions, the grieving, and the loss, before long they'd emerge on the other side. But what would be there for them? Maybe this could be a new chapter for the band. Become rejuvenated from the dark feelings, like soil enriched by crushed leaves.

Maybe he should call that number that Billy got. The tall, skinny dude didn't look like a typical record company type, either young and sporting clothes fashioned by Chance the Rapper or older and wearing $600 jeans and $200 T-shirts. He was in a low-level executive suit, black, no tie, extremely rumpled, as if he slept in it most nights of the week.

But you never know. They say the richest dudes in Bel Air dress in ripped jeans and huaraches. Maybe this guy was exactly what we need right now. Some money to record our songs, some paid promotion. Johnny imagined himself on stage in front of thousands of people, having his songs on people's lips, making an impact. Playing in front of ten, fifty, a hundred, when the music was happening and the crowd was into it was fantastic. The thought of that times ten, twenty caused a tingle to go up Johnny's neck.

"Hey Billy, you asleep?" They'd logged enough miles to know that if they drove for more than ten minutes, Billy might doze off. He could sleep at the drop of a hat. A magician would love him.

"Naw, mahn." Billy stretched his neck and opened his eyes. "Jus thinkin'."

"Me too. We oughta call that dude."

"OK," agreed Billy. "Yeah. Afta the funeral."

CHAPTER 20

Sometimes it feels like I'm stuck in this moment. As if time has stopped, and I'm looking at the world in stop-action photography, all in front of my eyes, images of men, women, boys and girls, trees, grass, sidewalks, buildings, homes, cars, bikes, scooters, everything that I can see has paused…

Then it's off. Not…quite…there. Half a beat off. Not detached but either behind or in front. Out of rhythm, the words halting, stop and start, the meaning all too slowly emerging or not emerging at all.

Is this unique to me? This time alteration, abbreviation, hesitation, procrastination.

Maybe my hearing's going. Maybe my sight too. Maybe I should have a drink.

Philip M. Cohen

CHAPTER 21

Earlier that night, not ten minutes after Billy had jumped into the SUV and drove off with Johnny, the doorbell at Lori's house rang.

"I'll get it," said Olivia.

"Thank you, dear," Lori said, her voice coming from the side bedroom.

"Billy?" said Olivia, turning the doorknob on the front door. "You forget something?" She pulled the door open and saw a man and a woman standing there.

"Ms. Feldon?" the woman said. She was five-foot-four, one-twenty, brown hair tied in a knot behind her head. "Do you remember me? Detective Lapidus." After a moment Olivia remembered. She and Lori had met Lapidus at the hospital, introduced to them by Officer Shields. She remembered the woman telling them that she was in charge of the investigation into Harry's shooting. Now it would be an investigation into murder.

"This is Detective Perry," Lapidus said. To her right, Perry nodded his head in greeting. A six-feet-three-inch-tall Black man, maybe thirty-five, dressed in a gray suit.

"Yeah, sure," said Olivia. "Hi."

"May we come in?" asked Perry.

"OK, but it's a mess," said Olivia.

"That's fine," said Lapidus. They walked inside and stood alongside the brown, overstuffed cloth sofa in the front room, Lori's sitting room.

"Do you want anything," asked Olivia, "Water, coffee?"

"No, we're fine. Just had Peet's." Lapidus cracked a forced smile at Olivia and opened a pad that she extracted from a brown leather handbag. "You know, Ms. Feldon, we'd like to talk to you about Harry. And we'd like the other Mrs. Feldon to join us." Lori's husband had been Olivia's father's brother, hence the same last name.

"She just went to lay down."

"No, that's OK," Lori said, appearing in the alcove at the end of the room twenty feet away, wearing a red bathrobe decorated with pictures of birds standing on branches and flying through the air. She sat on the couch next to Olivia and facing Lapidus and Perry.

"Now, you know, we were here after the ambulance took Mr. Feldon, your son," Lapidus said, indicating Lori, "to the hospital. We had a crime unit here and collected evidence. Well, you know, we didn't find much." She paused. "In the house, aside from Mr. Feldon's blood, all we found were some badly smudged fingerprints on the door to the bedroom. But not enough, I'm afraid, for an I.D."

Lori and Olivia nodded. It sounded like a dead end. They might never catch the murderers who killed Harry.

"So we're a bit stuck. It could've been a random break-in gone wrong," said Lapidus. "But we don't think so. The doctors pulled a .45-caliber bullet out of Mr. Feldon. Not unusual for criminals in L.A., but not usually what a burglar, even a professional, would carry. More often a .22 or .380, a smaller gun."

"If they carry one at all," added Perry.

"And these guys didn't act like burglars," continued Lapidus. "The place wasn't cleaned out. You haven't reported anything missing. Isn't that right?"

Lori replied, "Well, yes, that is right. I haven't noticed anything missing."

"Right," said Lapidus.

"So we were wondering, Mrs. Feldon," interjected Perry. "Could you tell us more about Harry, Mr. Feldon?"

"We know he lived here, didn't have a job, received disability from the state," said Lapidus. "But what did he do with himself? Did he have a love life? Friends beyond Ms. Feldon here and her friends with the musical group?"

"None that came over here," answered Lori. "He was a grown man. I didn't follow him around. If he went out, he'd sometimes tell me where he'd been, but sometimes not. I really didn't know any of his friends. Except for that boy Johnny. And, of course, Billy." She meekly smiled at Olivia at the mention of Billy's name.

"What about you, Miss," Perry asked Olivia. "Anything else you can think of? Maybe something he was into that he was keeping secret from everyone else?" Perry, Lapidus, and Lori all looked expectantly at Olivia. She racked her brain trying to come up with something.

"Oh, I really don't know," she said finally, exhaling a deep breath. "Except for always being broke 'cause of those stupid football bets."

Perry and Lapidus exchanged glances.

"He was into betting?" asked Lapidus. "Enough that he was always broke?"

"He was broke 'cause he was living on disability," said Lori.

"And he spent most of that money on betting," said

Olivia, the realization coming to her. "Maybe he owed the wrong person money."

"Perhaps," said Lapidus. She stood. "We'd like to take another look in Mr. Feldon's room. See if we find any indication of his betting and who he was betting with." She and Perry walked down the hall and disappeared around the corner.

An hour later, Lapidus and Perry were at the front door, exiting the house. She had told Lori and Olivia that they might be back with some pictures of local gamblers for them to possibly identify and handed Lori a card with an LAPD shield emblazoned on it along with "Connie Lapidus, Detective," and a phone number.

Not long after, Billy was back from the gig, staying the night with Olivia at Lori's place.

CHAPTER 22

J ohnny hated funerals. Even if it was a beautiful sunny
day, in the seventies, slight breeze blowing the leaves
from the trees. But funerals always felt dark and dreary
to him. Everyone dressed in dark clothes. The hushed conversations. The staid, awful ceremony as the priest, rabbi,
official presiding talked about someone they almost never
knew. Then standing over the grave and more solemn,
morbid prayers were said to an uncaring God. If he cared,
why create death? It was a sick joke, he thought.

Yet here he was. Sitting inside a stained-glass-windowed
building at the Forest Lawn cemetery, along with Shirlee,
Olivia, Lori, and the rest of the band. He had chosen not
to say anything. Everything he wanted to say about Harry
he had said last night at the club or in private to Lori. Poor
Harry. That unlucky fuck.

Johnny remembered his first funeral. And what led
up to it. He was nine, six inches shorter than all his class-
mates in third grade. But he didn't mind. He liked school
and especially liked Sally Marsh, a cute blond girl who sat
directly in front of him in class.

One day in February his mother wasn't home when he
got off the school bus in front of the apartment house where
he and his mother and father, Harriet and Eugene Watson,

lived in Woodland Hills on the southwestern end of the San Fernando Valley. He climbed the stairs to an empty second-story apartment, calling "Ma? You here?" Silence answered him. Until the phone rang. Johnny picked up the landline telephone. "Hello?" he answered.

"Johnny! Oh, Johnny." His mother's voice was constricted. She was crying. "It's Dad, honey."

Johnny's life was never the same. Johnny's father, a bus driver for the Metropolitan Transportation Authority in Los Angeles, had come home after his early morning shift, sat in his favorite La-Z-Boy recliner, fell asleep, and never awoke.

Two days later, Johnny was standing on a hill, overlooking the grave of his father. A light rain fell. The feel of the stiff white shirt and tie choking his throat. The sad and sympathetic looks from men and women who said they were his father's friends. The pats on his head. His mother crying into a handkerchief. He couldn't wait to get out of there, go home, get away.

It was like a chapter in a book had ended. An idyllic childhood, loving mother and father. Soccer and baseball. They were far from rich, but Johnny never was hungry. Always gifts on Christmas. That's how he remembered it. His mother had been reluctant to dispel his reverential memories of his father but did tell him eventually that things were not really as wholesome as he remembered, that there were loud, wall-shaking arguments, and door-slamming walkouts by Eugene.

Johnny never quite reconciled these tales with his memories. Because the second chapter was so distinctly different. His mother began to drink heavily. She had a series of jobs—secretary, grocery store clerk, waitress in a local diner—all of which ended the same: with Harriet sprawled on the sofa, passed out, emitting vodka fumes into the air. In the one-bedroom apartment they had moved into within six months of Eugene's death, Johnny slept on the sofa, and his mother had the bedroom. But on those too many nights that Harriet passed out on the couch, Johnny slept on the floor of her bedroom, the door closed to block the sound of her drunken snoring, not feeling comfortable sleeping in her bed.

She wasn't the only one to change. Johnny changed too. He was no longer the happy, alert, and studious kid he had been, the kid who had a room full of friends wherever he went. For a long time it appeared that he was in shock, not speaking to anyone, even friends he had been close with for years. His grades plummeted to new lows. School counselors called him into meetings where they spoke sympathetically to him, only to receive a blank stare back. He sleepwalked through grade school, the teachers passing him and moving him up to the next grade out of sympathy and routine.

Then at thirteen he was walking down Ventura Boulevard in Sherman Oaks. He had cut school that day and was wandering the street, stopping in frozen yogurt stores for free samples, and asking strangers for spare change. By this time his mother was on welfare, they used food stamps for groceries, and there was no money for any luxuries. He passed a large corner building with the faces of Jimi Hendrix and Tom Petty painted on the walls. Though heroes of another generation, Johnny was familiar with their music. His father, Eugene, used to sing along to Petty's "I Won't Back Down" whenever it came on the oldies radio station he loved. And Eugene played his CD copy of Hendrix's album "Axis: Bold as Love" so often Johnny could sing the words. Johnny opened the glass door to the building and entered the Guitar Center. Spread out in front of him was a toy store for musicians—a wall of amplifiers, a roomful of guitars, acoustic and electric, another room decked out in electronic keyboards and synthesizers. Upstairs was the drum room, with full sets on display, begging for someone to sit down and bash out a rhythm. And there was no shortage of players, musicians of all ages, men and women, young boys and girls, rat-tat-tatting on the drums or practice pads, pianos and organs tinkling and wailing, guitars jangling tunes familiar to Johnny and clusters of notes strung together in dense solos. It was the most fascinating place Johnny had ever seen. There were kids no older than he was really playing.

Johnny stood in wonder, staring at the delirium surrounding him when a teenage boy with long brown hair tied back into a ponytail asked him, "Can I help you? Need something?"

Johnny never needed anything so bad in his life. "Can I try a guitar?" he asked. The ponytailed boy, who introduced himself as Troy, led Johnny into the guitar room, pulled a Fender Mustang off the wall brackets it was hanging from and placed it in Johnny's hands. A guitar with a neck three-quarter the size of a Strat or Telecaster, it was perfect for still-growing, then-five-foot-six Johnny. He sat and strummed the strings.

"Let me give you your first lesson," said Troy. He showed Johnny how to play a basic E chord and then an A. Johnny twisted his fingers and pressed the strings down over and over again until the E and A chords rang out through the small amp that the guitar was plugged into. Time dissolved as Johnny played those two chords over and over. Finally, to his astonishment, Johnny thought it actually sounded like a song.

"How much?" he asked Troy, who had circled back and was watching Johnny.

"Normally four hundred," answered Troy. "But I can get it for you for three."

Johnny's face dissolved. Three hundred dollars?! Might just as well have said three thousand. No way he could imagine having that much money.

Troy saw his reaction and disappointment. It wasn't an unfamiliar sight in the store.

"Listen, kid," said Troy. "Too much money, huh?"

Johnny nodded, "Yeah, way too much."

"You could put some money down, and we'd hold it for you," said Troy. Johnny's mood didn't change. "No, huh?" Pause. "OK." He moved closer to Johnny and spoke in a quiet voice. "If you're lookin' for a cheap guitar, why don't you go to a pawnshop. If you're lucky you can find the same guitar or one good enough for a lot cheaper than here. Just don't tell anybody I said so. I wanna keep my job."

Johnny's eyes brightened, and he grinned from ear to ear. "Thanks, Troy!" he called out as he ran out of the store. There were plenty of pawn shops on Sherman Way in Reseda, just down the street from where he and his mom lived.

He was a guitar man from that day on. Johnny placed twenty-five dollars, which he had taken from his mother's bedside drawer, in the hand of the old, unshaven man at the pawn shop as a down payment on an Epiphone guitar. A bargain, the old man had said, for a hundred bucks. Johnny did whatever he could to earn enough money for that guitar. He was too young for a regular job, but he was determined and knocked on the doors of everyone in the apartment house where they lived, asking his neighbors if they had any jobs he could do. He swept the courtyard, walked dogs, painted walls, even figured out how to fix a leaky faucet. After a busy month, Johnny had that Epiphone and played it until his fingers bled. Before long he was playing and singing along to "I Won't Back Down."

That seemed so long ago to Johnny now as he stood over Harry's grave and tossed a guitar pick down onto the pile of dirt covering the coffin. Billy walked up to him.

"Shitty day, mahn. Days like today makes ya…ah…jus don' know."

"Know what ya mean," replied Johnny. He and Billy walked down the hill, passing by other groups of people, strangers. All united in one thing, thought Johnny morbidly. Shirlee was standing in the parking lot, next to the Civic and alongside a man and a woman.

"Billy, Johnny. These officers want to speak with you," said Shirlee. "About Harry."

Lapidus introduced herself and Perry as detectives, explaining that they had spoken to Lori and Olivia the evening before and were hoping for more background on Harry, his habits, and particularly his gambling.

"Gamblin'?" said Billy. "Mahn was always busted. Was he eva payin' for his own drinks?"

"Maybe that's why," said Perry. "Did he ever act unusual? Ever see him with strangers?"

"No, he was usually alone," said Johnny. "He did flake out on us the other night at the club. Took off. Said he was leaving with some guys he knew. But I never saw them."

"He was also all over me the other night about my old man's old business address," said Billy, recalling the peculiar conversation. Billy told them of that conversation, that his late father had been a dentist with an office in Tarzana, but had a place before he was born somewhere in or around downtown.

Lapidus made notes in her pad, took their personal info, and gave them business cards. "Call if you think of anything else. We'll be in touch." She and Perry turned to leave, walking toward a black Crown Vic parked nearby.

"Hey, Miss, er, Detective," Billy called after them. "Any chance you can check out who messed up my place the other night? After the cops left I haven't heard a word." The officers stopped, and Billy told them of the break-in at his apartment and how nothing had been taken. He showed them Officer Garcia's business card, which he had kept in his wallet.

"All right," said Lapidus. "I'll call Garcia. Maybe it's a coincidence. But maybe not." She and Perry drove off, leaving Shirlee, Billy, and Johnny in the cemetery parking lot.

"Maybe we should speak to your mom, Billy," suggested Johnny. "Harry was awful eager to get that info about your dad's old place. Maybe she'll remember something."

"She can't remember her own name most of the time," said Billy. They piled into the Civic, and Johnny drove down the driveway onto the long street bordering the cemetery.

"It's worth a try," said Shirlee.

"Oh, OK, guess so," agreed Billy. "B'sides, I owe her a visit."

CHAPTER 23

Clifton eyed the menu, while Manny sipped a freshly poured cup of coffee. They were sitting at a table near the window at the House of Pies. Located on the east end of Franklin Avenue at Vermont Avenue, it was situated perfectly between the apartments of Hollywood and the old mansions of Los Feliz, between the young and the old, the well off and the just getting by. And the coffee shop, a neighborhood institution for over five decades, attracted them all.

"I love this place," said Manny. He had decided on a slice of coconut cream before he sat down, having eyed the slices on other patrons' plates. He scanned the room, lingering on the young girls wearing shorts and tight T-shirts.

"I'll have a slice of blueberry," Clifton said to a waiter stopping by their table. Manny gave his order. "What the hell is Brick doing out there?" They could see Brick through the plate glass window. He was pacing, walking back and forth in the parking lot as if he was on an exercise regimen.

Outside, Brick's cell phone rang. He answered, nearly dropping the phone as he pulled it from his pocket.

"Yeah," he said. "It's me."

"All right, Brick," came the deep baritone voice on the other end. "You know that you've been wasting my time and patience. Do I have to remind you that you owe me?"

"No. No, sir," stammered Brick. "I know the score. I'm gonna get it for you."

"'Cause I'd hate to have to end our working relationship."

Brick felt the threat throughout his body, his neck hairs bristling, his stomach knotting. The line went dead. He walked into the coffee shop, fell into the booth alongside Clifton, and brusquely told a passing waitress to bring him coffee.

"Have some pie," said Manny, scooping a bite into his mouth.

"I don't want fuckin' pie, you moron." He couldn't believe he had to deal with this idiot. He wasn't even sure he could depend on Manny when things got tough. But he sure did look the part.

"What's the word?" asked Clifton quietly. "We really oughta lay low for a while. Considering."

"What are you worrying about?" said Brick. "Nobody knows nothing. And we have to find that address. And soon." He had a plan. Get that boy alone under the pretense of giving them a record deal and sweat it out of him. Brick bolted up, exited the building, and began walking the parking lot again. He dialed Billy's cell phone number.

"Ya mahn. Not here. Ya know what t'do," was the voice mail message.

"Billy," Brick said exuberantly. "Hey guy. It's Rick, buddy. I'd love to get together and discuss a deal for you. Give me a call back." He left Billy his phone number on the burner phone he was using. He'd lose it soon enough.

Brick owed the boss man fifty large, and the vig was growing each day. But if he got the address he was clean. Those damn Rams. If they had only won the Super Bowl. He had taken too many bets on the Pats without laying off enough to cover any potential losses and protect himself. A goddamn rookie mistake. But he had been so sure. Inside information, my ass. That equipment manager for the Pats, claiming Brady could hardly walk. Jesus. And now he was into the man, and a sword was hanging over his head. Well, this stops now. Brick waved Clifton and Manny out of the coffee shop, and they sped into Hollywood.

CHAPTER 24

Billy entered the spacious lobby of the Actors Fund Retirement Home in Woodland Hills. Located near the Fallbrook Avenue exit of the 101, the home was on the western edge of Ventura Boulevard in the San Fernando Valley, the long street that originated in Hollywood as Cahuenga Boulevard and meandered up over the hills into the San Fernando Valley. Cahuenga became Ventura, a major thoroughfare through the length of the valley and, ten miles later, in front of the Actors Home, the streets leading into the Santa Monica Mountains behind.

Billy knew the layout. He passed by the front desk, saying hello to Johanna, the young Latina woman who helped visitors. He nodded to Barry, the security guard. They knew him.

His mother had lived here for a year. After Billy's dad died, she had managed by herself, running errands, maintaining a household, and working at the pet store down the street from their condo in Tarzana. But Billy knew she was slipping. He'd find her staring out the window of the condo, mumbling to herself. She'd ask Billy what year it was. Sometimes she didn't even recognize him, calling him Ted, his father's name. After a couple of years, it became too severe to ignore. Afraid to leave her alone, he researched retirement homes on the internet, calling the places he thought sounded best, the ones with full medical care as well as being top rated. He had remembered his mother telling him about her time as a young woman acting in commercials, portraying an eager housewife pouring Folgers and the wife of a couple with big smiles on their faces in front of a house with a "Sold" sign over a Coldwell Banker sign. Billy had contacted the Actors Home and filled out the paperwork, embellishing her career sufficiently for admittance.

It wasn't an easy place to visit for Billy. He knew this was the last place many of the people here would ever live. There were activities, movie nights, outings to restaurants, performances by the residents. But Mary, Billy's mom, wasn't able to join in. She mostly stayed in her small room, often forgetting to eat, visited only by staff and occasionally Billy.

Billy wandered down the long hallway with green walls adorned with photos of semi-celebrities who lived or once lived here. He heard music playing from one room, a Beatles tune Billy recognized. Voices came from another room, a half-hearted argument over cards.

The door to room 412 was open. His mother, Mary Edgars Bates, was sitting by the window, looking out intently, humming to herself. Billy walked over, bent, and kissed her on the forehead.

"Hi, Ma. How are you?" he greeted her.

"Have I missed lunch again, doctor?" she asked, startled out of her reverie.

"No, Ma. It's me. Billy."

"Billy? I don't know any Billy. Go away." She turned her head back toward the window.

He took her hands in his. "Ma, you remember me, don't you? It's your son, William."

Philip M. Cohen

She looked at him with suspicion that gradually faded into a dim awareness. "William? My little William. Oh he was so cute when he was small. All the other mothers were so jealous, crowding around the stroller, oohing and aahing. Did you know him?"

"That's me, Ma." Billy looked for any sign of recognition. But her alertness faded. "Ma? Mary?" he tried without getting any response other than her softly humming an indecipherable tune.

A middle-aged Black woman stuck her head inside the doorway. "Mary? Mrs. Bates? How are we doing today?" She stepped in. Billy knew her from earlier visits.

"She doesn't know who I am today, Ms. Lenore," said Billy, standing and letting her get closer to his mother.

"Mary," she said. "Mary, do you know who this is? This is your son. It's Billy, your son with Ted, your husband."

"Ted?" She turned to him, her face lighting up. "Teddy, you're home." Mary reached her hand out, grasped Billy's hand, and pulled him into an embrace. "Oh, Teddy," she said coquettishly. "You're home early from West Moore just for me." She kissed her son as if they were lovers, hard and passionate before Billy was able to untangle himself.

"Mom! It's me, Billy. Not dad. Not Ted!"

"Not Ted?" Mary looked up at Billy, then turned to Ms. Lenore. "Not Teddy? Oh." She began to cry.

"Mary," said Ms. Lenore, holding Mary's hand and speaking firmly but sympathetically, "you're all right. Everything's all right now." She patted Mary's hand, calming her. Mary's expression eased from anguish to blank in seconds. She turned, hands still being held by Ms. Lenore, and faced the window, humming again.

Ms. Lenore stood and led Billy toward the door.

"You might as well go, Billy," she said. "She's not having a good day today."

Billy looked back at his mother. A great sadness welled up in his chest, and he strained to stop from crying. He never had the chance to ask her about his father's old office.

"OK. I'll come back soon. Thank you." He walked down the hallway to the exit. It was a typical, bright, no-cloud-in–the-sky Southern California day, but the harrowing visit with his mother replayed itself in Billy's mind. She thought I was my dad, he thought. Again. But this time she actually kissed me! Oh man. He physically shivered in revulsion. But what was that she said? About being home from the office? Something about West Moore?

Johnny was waiting on the street, standing next to the Civic, drinking a Mountain Dew.

"How'd it go? Did she remember anything?"

"Naw, she was completely out of it," Billy replied. "It was awful." They slid into the car and Johnny started the engine. "Ever heard of West Moore? She was goin' on about my dad and asked if he was home from West Moore."

"No." Johnny pulled over from the curb. Billy's phone played a piano blues riff, his ringtone.

"Yeah," he answered. "Who dis?"

"Billy, Billy the Kid!" the voice said. "Hey, it's Rick. From the club."

"Yeah, hey, Rick." Billy put his hand over the mouthpiece and told Johnny it was the record guy he met at Slim's. "What's de word der, Rick?"

"I think we should get together and discuss recording your band, Billy. I haven't heard anything like you boys in years."

"Yeah, OK," said Billy, his gloom lifting slightly at the prospect of recording. "Sure. Me and Johnny can meet. Hear whacha have t'say." He nodded at Johnny, they had a fish on the line.

"Great, great. How 'bout we meet at the Federal? It's near the club on Lankershim. Tomorrow at five."

"Yeah, the Federal at five, sure. See ya." Billy hung up. "Well, whaddya think a' that?" he asked Johnny. "A record deal maybe. Get some do-re-mi happenin'." He grinned and rubbed his hands together.

"Don't spend that money yet." Johnny laughed. "Let's see if he pays for drinks." They drove east on Ventura Boulevard. The day seemed much sunnier to Billy now.

At the same time, Brick was slipping his phone into his jacket pocket in the back seat of the Escalade, parked across the boulevard from the Actors Home.

CHAPTER 25

It isn't always so easy. Oh yes, the words can just spring from my head and through my voice, a transit without thought or conscious comprehension. And the music just materializes, my hands moving effortlessly over the strings, one note cascading into the next, the next, and next, the progression forming neatly, smoothly. Until there it is, as if it was always there. Born whole. A bouncing baby tune. A joyful sound. A melody with no need for remedy. A luscious lyric with every spirit within it. Sometimes. Yeah, I agree—sometimes. So pure, unadulterated, uncensored, boundless.

But other times…oh lawd, other times, the universe conspires against me. A chord progression meanders into a hole, ending nowhere but dissonance. Or worse, nowhere except where it's been before.

And the lyrics sound as if a five-year-old is rhyming moon, spoon, June, tune. Meanings dissipate; imagery fades out of the picture. Like a watercolor left in the sun. Hoping the rains don't come and wash the picture completely away, blanking whatever was lurking, hungry to emerge, yet not strong enough to announce itself to the world.

There is the middle ground. Workmanlike. Slow and steady. One note leading gradually to the next. A sequence of notes and chords leading to the next, hanging finally together in an acceptable and satisfying sum of its parts. And one word leading eventually to another. As…if…they…were…destined to abut each other, support each other, enhance each other, embrace each other, fulfill each other. Not that it can stop there. It has to be worked and reworked. And undone and done again. Then start once more and end again, start again, add, subtract, augment, refine. Pressing for that diamond, that definitive gem of an idea made real, no longer abstract, no longer a thin wisp of a musical breath whispering in the air. No longer a cute or clever turn of phrase simply elongated into three verses, a chorus and a bridge. Or four verses, or five, six, or seven. So sturdy and secure, an entire roomful of souls can find it and make it theirs.

Sing along. If you sing along, I'll know you're there. Sing along, I'll know you've heard it. Sing along, I'll know you understand. Sing along, I'll know I was here.

CHAPTER 26

I t wasn't night yet as Johnny parked his car on the street in
front of the Federal, a refurbished restaurant/bar/club in
a refurbished section of North Hollywood. Long an area
of low-income housing, car dealerships, and Latino gang
territory that the LAPD preferred to avoid after dark, in
recent years the area, renamed Noho, had been gentrified
and transformed by hip clubs, coffee shops, new housing
developments, and the crown jewel of the area, the Television Academy, where the history of television is celebrated
and special events, such as premieres and seminars on TV,
are held. Not that the low-income housing had disappeared
completely. It'd just been pushed a little farther north, with
Burbank Boulevard only blocks away a dividing line.

Johnny and Billy exited the Civic and entered the Federal. They peered through the low lighting and saw a bar
in front of them, a few early evening patrons drinking and
talking. A half dozen tables were spread along the wall. Billy
didn't see Rick at either the tables or bar. Standing beside
an entryway alongside the tables was a hostess stand, where
a young, dark-haired woman greeted them.

"Table for two?" the hostess asked.

"Ah, we meetin someone. A skinny dude named Rick?"
said Billy.

"Yes, he's already here. Right this way." She walked through the entryway, leading Johnny and Billy past more tables and an empty stage in an adjoining room and up a curving flight of stairs. Three small wrought iron tables were arranged on the balcony overlooking the dining floor below. At one table sat Rick.

"Billy!" he called out, standing to embrace Billy in a bro hug and pumping his hand. "And you must be Johnny." He reached out to grasp Johnny's hand. "We're gonna do great things, boys."

They all sat, and a waitress took their orders, beers all around.

"So," began Brick, rubbing his hands eagerly. "How long you boys been playing?"

Johnny told him the story of how he and Billy had met, how they had met Beans through a Craigslist ad a few years ago, and how Beans had been dating Frank's older sister. Beans often heard him woodshedding in his room, playing his bass to Van Halen tracks, and suggested to Johnny that they give him a try.

"Yeah, mahn. De rest be histry," added Billy. "Now you. What's wit your label?"

"Yeah," said Johnny, "and where do we fit?"

"Right in the pocket," grinned Brick. "It's a new label. We're getting funding from a Chinese venture capital firm. You know they're all over Hollywood these days. We haven't even put up a website yet. But you boys can be our premiere act. We'll focus all our energies helping you and introducing you to the public."

"What about recording?" asked Johnny.

"Absolutely," said Brick. "We'll get you into a studio right away. First we have to work out the details of the deal.

You guys have a lawyer?" They shook their heads. "Doesn't matter. It'll be a simple contract. Money to record, we'll promote you, everybody'll be happy." He raised a beer in a toast. Johnny and Billy picked up their glasses off the table a few inches. "OK. I'll put together the deal and get it to you in the next couple of days. That work for you?"

"Sure," said Billy. Johnny nodded his consent.

"OK," said Brick. "I gotta go. Work, work, work. I'll give you a call soon, Billy. It's gonna be great." He stood, placed a one hundred dollar bill on the table, clasped hands with each in turn, and descended the staircase. They watched him go, draining their beers and signaling the waitress for another round.

"Is fantastic!" said Billy, enthusiastically smacking the table with both hands. "We goin' to record and be big stahs!"

"Maybe," said Johnny, taking a sip of beer. "But isn't this too good to be true? I mean, I know the music is good, but a stranger starting a new record company laying out money on an unknown band? There's better ways to make money. We've been at it for years and have to work those other crummy jobs to earn a living."

"You think you're gonna have to be a security guard protecting no one in an office building forever? Or me selling T-shirts and rolling papers to kids at Active?" Billy replied. "Mahn, it pay the rent, but it's nowhere. This could be our big break."

"Yeah, OK," said Johnny. "Let's see what the offer is. We can take it from there."

By the time they finished their beers and left the bar, it was night. The lights on the boulevard shone down on the pot dispensary and comedy theater next door. Johnny drove away, heading for Reseda to drop Billy off.

"How's your place shaping up?" he asked Billy, entering the westbound 101 Freeway. "You clean up the mess?"

"Yeah, mostly," said Billy. "Livie done most. But there's nothing new from de cops. Guess they figure it too small time to bodda wit."

They drove on, taking an off-ramp after a few miles. Billy opened the door and exited when they stopped. He walked toward the apartment building, and Johnny drove away, planning to meet tomorrow night after work for rehearsal. Neither one saw the Escalade parking across the street moments later.

Billy fumbled for his door key, feeling the effects of the beers. He pressed the buzzer, thinking that Livie letting him in was easier than finding the damn key.

"Hello," came Olivia's voice through the intercom. Before Billy could answer a hand was placed over his mouth, and he was yanked off his feet. He struggled and shook, fighting to break the grip of the hands carrying him into the street. He was thrown into the Escalade.

"Hey, wha de…!" Before Billy could say anything else or yell for help, a strip of duct tape was placed over his mouth by a sandy-haired man. The sandy-haired man, big but not nearly as huge as the driver wheeling the car away from the curb, bound his hands and feet. Billy looked up, making incomprehensible but angry sounds through the tape. A skinny guy turned in his seat up front. Billy stopped squirming and tried to speak, a sick realization dawning.

"Take it easy, Billy," said Brick. "I said I'd be in touch soon. So maybe it's a little sooner than you thought."

Back at the apartment house, Olivia called into the intercom. "Hello? Hello? Billy? Is that you? Billy?" The anonymous sound of cars driving past on the street on the other end filled her with dread.

CHAPTER 27

"He never got home," Olivia told Johnny early the next morning. Johnny had told her of dropping Billy off right in front of their place a little after eight. "Where could he have gone?"

It wasn't like Billy, thought Johnny. Sure, he was spaced out at times, liking his booze and pot, but he was also a homebody. Aside from playing music, his favorite thing was to be in his own little crib, smoking a joint, listening to music, or watching TV. He never left town. For being such a crazy White Rasta, Billy was basically a down-to-earth guy.

"Did you call his cell?" Johnny asked.

"No answer. I left a message on his voice mail. Told him to call me right away."

"Call all his friends. And the old age home where his mom lives. Maybe he decided to visit overnight." Johnny knew that was unlikely, but he was grasping at straws. "I have to go to work. But call me on my cell if you find out anything."

Johnny hung up and dressed in his Universal Private Security Services uniform. He quickly donned his blue pants, shirt, and pseudo cop hat. He pinned the "UPSS" badge on, buckled his holster, fitting in the .40-caliber Glock 22 revolver. Rather than go to college, Johnny knew he wanted to be a musician. But he was realistic too. At his school guidance counselor's suggestion, he hesitantly agreed to train for three months after the last year of high school with this security firm. To his surprise, he enjoyed the training. Basic martial arts and surveillance, how to shoot—it was exciting. It was the job, unfortunately, that wasn't. Standing around all day in a big office building on Wilshire Boulevard in Beverly Hills, feeling like a weirdo, trying to look menacing, yet protective at the same time, getting mocking looks from the Beverly Hills cops who occasionally came by. And the pay was nothing much. Little more than minimum wage. But it was better than delivering packages all over Southern California, his last job before this. Or scooping ice cream at the BK. Besides, Shirlee liked a man in uniform. Playing cops and robbers was one of her favorite things.

"Lookin' hot, baby," Shirlee said, coming up behind him and looping her fingers inside his belt. He swung around and twisted her arm behind her.

"I'm gonna have to use all reasonable force on you," he whispered in her ear.

"Hmm, do it," she squealed. She spun, yanked on his belt, pressing up against him, and kissed him hard on the mouth.

"OK, girl," said Johnny after they unclenched. "I gotta get to work. If you hear anything from Olivia about Billy, let me know."

"Maybe we should call the cops. With everything that's been going on, maybe they should know."

"Maybe. Let's give it until this evening. Right now they won't take it seriously. He's only been gone less than twelve hours."

"I guess," agreed Shirlee.

"I'll see you tonight." He opened the door, heading for the street.

"Don't be late, Officer." She licked her lips suggestively as Johnny closed the door behind him. What a delicious character, he thought. He hopped into the Civic and drove toward the 405 Freeway, heading over the mountains toward Wilshire Boulevard.

Back in the apartment, Shirlee was restless. She still hadn't found a job, and it was too much to ask Johnny to hang around all day and play with her. Maybe she should call Olivia. She sounded worried sick earlier. She found her phone under one of the cushions on the sofa and dialed.

"Hello? Shirlee? That you?" Olivia answered on the first ring.

"Hey Livie. Was thinkin' about you," said Shirlee. "How 'bout some company?" She told Olivia she'd be there soon. She hung up, grabbed her purse, and headed to the bus stop on Van Nuys. Shirlee knew it was a long wait for a bus and then a long ride, but it was better than waiting in the apartment.

CHAPTER 23

They rolled, bumped, stopped, and started for a half hour, although Billy thought it was longer as he was jostled from side to side and forward and back. What a lousy driver, he thought. And what the hell is this? Why would Rick grab me like this? Is this some sick Hollywood negotiating tactic to get them to sign their music away?

Rick was staring at him, a weasel's cunning emanating from his eyes. He hadn't seen this from Rick before. And who were these other two characters? Both big, big like football players, big enough to be bouncers at any club in town.

The vehicle bumped over a barrier in the road and stopped. Billy heard a metal garage door opening, and they were going backwards, pulling in. The side door swung open, and Billy saw a nondescript space, gray walls twelve feet high. The sandy-haired man reached in, took Billy by the arm, and dragged him out of the Escalade, standing him up. He ripped the tape off Billy's mouth.

"Now, Billy," the sandy-haired guy said. "My name is Cliff. I help your buddy here with problems. You know about problems?" He waited for Billy to nod his head once. "Sure. Course ya do. Well, we got ourselves a problem that you can help us with. Do you think you can do that?" Billy nodded yes again. "Good, good. Now you remember your dad, of course. You know he didn't treat you all that good, right? Busy with his work, no time for a kid like you. Right?"

Billy stared at him. What was this guy talking about? Playing amateur psychologist with him after dragging him off the streets? And one thing he now knew for sure—Rick wasn't his buddy.

"Now you don't owe your pops nothin'," continued Clifton. "There's no need for you to hide what you know from us because we're on your side."

"That's right," said Brick. "Be cooperative, and we can still get you that record deal."

A record deal? Wha the fuck? A record deal was the furthest thing from Billy's mind right now. He didn't know what these guys wanted, but it wasn't to sign Conflict and make them rock stars.

"Now, Billy," said Brick, circling around to face him, the driver and Cliff to either side of Billy. "There's some information I need to get from you."

"Information? What information? What is this, Rick?" said Billy.

"Yeah. Now listen," said Brick. "Tell me what I need to know, and I drop you off back home, and we go on our merry way. OK?" Billy weakly nodded his head. "But don't tell me and…"

Cliff swung his arm and smacked Billy in the face with the back of his hand, lifting him off his feet and onto the floor.

"You get the picture, don't you, Billy?" said Brick, bending down and straightening Billy's shirt. Billy weakly nodded again, sniffling back blood dripping from his nose. "Good. Good. Clifton, give our guest a seat." Clifton placed a wooden folding chair beside Billy, lifted him off the ground, and placed him aggressively on the seat.

"OK, then," began Brick. "I need you to remember where your old man used to work. You give me the address, and that's the end of it." He waved his arm as if everything that was happening was a minor inconvenience easily rectified.

"The ad…address?" stammered Billy. "Wha add…" The address, he thought. The same address that Harry was asking about. Before he was killed. Billy looked up into Rick's eyes with newly blossoming fear. "Er, I don't know of any…" He never saw Clifton's backhand coming, slapping him, sending him sprawling again on the concrete floor

"Yes, you do, you little shit, the address. The one downtown," insisted Brick, bending down and speaking the words inches from Billy's face.

"But I don't know," said Billy desperately. "I wasn't even born then."

"You better remember something your dad said then," said Brick. "Or else my friend here will have to help you remember."

Clifton reached down, put Billy back in the chair, then reached back to strike Billy again but stopped at the sound of a cell phone ringing.

"What the…," Brick said impatiently. He answered the phone. "Yeah? Yes. Yes, sir. Real soon. In the garage. Right. As soon as I know. Yes, sir." He hung up. "Shit. We're running out of time." He nodded at Clifton who knocked Billy out of the chair with a smash to the face. Billy hit the ground hard, smacking his head, and lost consciousness.

"You fuckin' animal!" hissed Brick belligerently. "We need him alive and talking. You and Manny make sure he's OK. I'll be back." He opened the pedestrian door that was part of the larger garage door and stormed out, leaving Clifton and Manny with Billy. They exchanged glances.

"He's running scared," said Clifton. He and the huge Escalade driver, Manny, lifted the unconscious Billy off the floor and laid him on a tattered couch in the corner of the garage.

"Yeah," said Manny. "And that ain't good for nobody. Not good at all."

CHAPTER 23

Shirlee reached Olivia's apartment after an hour's bus ride. It would have taken fifteen minutes by car. Public transportation is sorely lacking in this town, thought Shirlee. She buzzed the intercom at Olivia's apartment house, and the intercom echoed the sound a moment later, unlocking the front door. Shirlee opened it and stepped through.

"Shirlee. Come on up." Olivia called from the landing above. Shirlee took the elevator up. They embraced and went into the apartment.

"Looks nice," said Shirlee, looking around the small apartment. "Can't even tell."

"Took enough work. Something to drink? Joint?" Olivia offered. She went to a drawer and pulled a small glass jar container with the label Dream Catcher, took out a large bud of pot, and pinched some into a glass pipe. She offered the first hit to Shirlee.

"Thanks for coming by," Olivia said, accepting the pipe back and inhaling. "It's been a tough few days. First the apartment. Then Harry. Poor Lori. I'm going back over there later. And now Billy is missing."

"Is Lori OK? Have you heard anything from the cops about any of this?"

"Lori's doing as well as you'd expect. No, not a peep from the cops. They said they'd call if they found something, but they never called."

"What about school? Aren't you missing classes? You gotta keep up if you're gonna be our mini-lawyer."

"One or two. That's OK. I can make it up. Most of the work is online anyway," said Olivia. She was taking a paralegal course at UCLA Extension in Westwood. A year part time, and she'd be a paralegal. Rather than three years full time to be an attorney.

Shirlee's phone rang. "It's Johnny," she said to Olivia. "Hey, honey," she said into the phone.

"Hi. Where are you?" Johnny said. "Maybe you should go to Olivia's. Keep her company. Hopefully Billy'll show his face soon."

"She's with me now," called out Olivia, loud enough to be heard through the phone in Shirlee's hand.

"Yeah. And no Billy," said Shirlee. She sucked on the pipe, inhaled, and exhaled a billow of smoke.

"Don't get too high," said Johnny, recognizing the sound. "I have to get back. But see if you can find a West Moore Street downtown."

"West Moore?" asked Shirlee. "What's that?"

Maybe something to do with all of this, thought Johnny. "It's something Billy's mom said. His dad's old office maybe. Gotta go. See you at home."

"Where's your laptop?" asked Shirlee. Olivia found the Lenovo computer on the kitchen table, carried it over to the couch, and booted it up. Shirlee looked over her shoulder.

"West Moore Street," Olivia said as she typed the address into Google Maps. An area between Glendale and downtown Los Angeles came up as Moore Street. "Maybe this is it." She wrote the directions on a slip of paper. "Let's get an Uber." She pressed the app on her phone and entered the destination. "Five minutes away." They exited the apartment, went downstairs, and waited for the car.

Five minutes later a blue Prius with Uber and Lyft stickers on the windshield stopped by the curb.

"Olivia?" the female driver asked through the passenger side window. The women climbed in, and drove east toward Glendale.

CHAPTER 30

Billy opened his eyes to see Clifton, the guy who had first sweet talked him and then beaten him unconscious, staring into his face. Behind him stood the other guy who was built like a brick wall.

"You OK, kid?" Clifton asked.

Everything that had happened flooded into Billy's mind. He felt dizzy, sick to his stomach.

"Easy, kid," said Clifton, seeing the panic and nauseated look in Billy's face. "I don't want to keep smacking you around. You look like a cool kid. No. This'll all be over if you just tell Brick what he wants to know."

"I...I don't know," said Billy. Thoughts of his father getting home from work came to his mind. His dad coming through the door, his mother stirring a martini for him. "How was work?" "Another tough day." But that was all when his father had an office in Tarzana.

"I was too young," said Billy.

"Well, you better think hard and think quick or you're not gonna get any older." Brick had come back with a 9 mm Beretta in his hand. He waved it in front of Billy. "Where the fuck was your old man's office?!"

West Moore. His mom had said, "You're back from West Moore."

"West Moore," mumbled Billy. "West Moore Street."

"Let's go," commanded Brick. "We're gonna find this place now."

Clifton picked Billy up from the couch and moved him through the garage door back into the Escalade. He sat in the back sandwiched between Brick and Clifton.

"GPS it," said Brick, pointing at the traffic guide on the dashboard.

"Right," said Manny, typing the street name in as he drove. "There's a Moore Street in Glendale leading into one in L.A. nearby."

"That must be it," said Brick. "All right. Finally. Was that so hard?" He stared daggers at Billy. "Musicians," he said scornfully.

CHAPTER 31

The blue Prius exited the Ventura Freeway on Glendale Avenue, went for a mile, turned right and then a left after another 900 yards. The 2200 block of Moore Street. The potholed single-lane street ran between rows of buildings built between the world wars in which resided small grocery stores, a Goodwill clothing outlet, and other struggling retail shops. Gentrification hadn't hit this area yet.

Shirlee and Olivia got out and walked. They weren't sure what they were looking for, but doing something was better than sitting at home and waiting endlessly for the police.

"Maybe there's an old medical office building around here," suggested Shirlee. She was doubtful as she scanned the street. Signs in Spanish, English, and Armenian mingled together inside and outside the stores. She couldn't imagine this being an area where Billy's dad had a dental office. But it was part of L.A. Everywhere in this town changed constantly. It was possible. "How long is this street?"

"It goes on for about a mile, but I don't see anything," said Olivia. "Why don't we split up? You go that way..." pointing north, "and I'll go this way." She walked south. "If you see anything," she said over her shoulder, "...call."

Olivia looked into every store she passed, gazing into the windows, trying to detect any sign that this store, this

102   *Philip M. Cohen*

shop, this shuttered building might have once been a dentist's office. She covered a dozen blocks, but none of the retail shops were likely candidates. She was becoming discouraged, thinking they were never going to find it, until she spotted a beige three-story building across the street with a sign out front advertising "Professional Offices." She excitedly called Shirlee and told her what she had found and to meet her there.

Olivia entered the building and looked at the worn directory. Two general practice doctors, one obstetrician, one lawyer, and one dentist. The rest of the offices showed vacancies. She climbed the stairs to the second floor and entered an office with a plaque on the door reading "South Glendale Dental." Inside, a Hispanic woman sat in the waiting room, calming her young daughter. Olivia walked up to the reception desk, where a Latina with an abundance of flowing black hair and a name tag that read "Gloria" looked up.

"Um, excuse me," began Olivia. "But has this always been a dentist's office?"

"What?" said Gloria. "Do you have an appointment?" She looked down into her schedule.

"No. No, I was wondering how long this office has been a dentist's office."

"Gee, I don't know. Doctor Marino has been here, oh, twelve years, I think," Gloria said. "I've been with him for three now."

Not long enough, thought Olivia. "What about before Doctor Marino?"

"Oh, I really don't know. You should talk to the building management company, Servritt Management." Gloria wrote a number on a pad of paper that had two unicorns leaping into the air under the words "From the Office of Dr. Marino, DDS" and handed the top sheet to Olivia.

"Thank you," she said, exiting the office, walking down the stairs, and leaving the building. Shirlee hadn't gotten there yet. She noticed a black Escalade parked fifty feet down the street and two men walking toward her. She passed them and looked at the vehicle.

Inside the car, Billy was sitting in the back seat with Manny up front, switching stations on the radio. Brick had found the only office building in this area on the internet, and he and Clifton had left the car to check it out. Clifton had tied Billy's hands together with a plastic tie. Billy looked forlornly at the outside world through the back seat window, wondering if he was ever going to get out of this, when he thought he saw a vision.

"Livie?!" he called.

"What?" said Manny, turning toward him.

"Olivia! Olivia!" Billy yelled, banging on the car window.

Outside Olivia heard the commotion in the car. She saw him. "Billy! Billy!" she cried.

"What the…," said Manny. He saw who Billy was yelling to. This was bad. They were creating a scene. The police might be called. He leaped from the car, circled around, and grabbed Olivia. She swung her legs, kicking Manny, who hoisted her into the air, pinning her arms. Olivia twisted her body, opened her mouth wide, and bit Manny on the cheek.

"Bitch!" cried Manny, throwing her onto the ground. He advanced on her. Olivia was on her knees, gasping for air. Manny, as big as a bear, reached down to pick her up again when he was knocked to the ground from behind. Billy, his hands still tied together, reared back and swung his leg as hard and as fast as he could. Billy almost toppled forward, but his foot connected with Manny's head, which snapped back and smashed into the concrete sidewalk.

"Come on," said Olivia. "Run." She sprang to her feet.

"This way," said Billy. He pushed Olivia into the Escalade.

"A knife, something," pleaded Billy, turning to show Olivia his tied hands. She hurriedly rummaged through her purse, found a small cuticle scissors, and snipped the plastic apart. Billy jumped behind the wheel. The keys were still in the ignition, the radio still playing, Willie Nelson singing about being on the road again. Billy stomped on the accelerator, and the car leaped from the curb.

Behind them came shouts and the sounds of gunshots. Two panging sounds echoed through the car.

"Get down," yelled Billy. They heard another two shots, but they were out of range within moments.

"Stop! Stop!" yelled Olivia.

"What? We gotta…"

"Shirlee! There's Shirlee!"

Billy screeched the car to a stop as Olivia swung the car door open, calling Shirlee's name. Shirlee was stunned, hesitated, and stared at the Escalade in confusion. But Olivia reached down and yanked her inside. Billy zoomed off.

CHAPTER 32

"Why were you…"
  "What happened to…"
  "Who were those…"

Billy, Olivia, and Shirlee all fired off questions at the same time, their adrenaline pumping. Billy told them about Brick/Rick and how he had been grabbed right outside his apartment. Olivia told them of the information she had gotten in Dr. Marino's office and about the Servritt Management Company.

Billy raced through Glendale, navigating tight turns, his wrists stiff and showing red circles from the plastic ties. He maneuvered onto the 134 Freeway and headed west.

"We can't go home," said Olivia. "They know where we live."

"My place," said Shirlee. "I think it'll be OK there. I'll let Johnny know we found you."

"Yeah, your place be cool," said Billy, his Rasta self resurfacing. "Maybe they have me old man's old place now, they'll lay off."

Shirlee dialed Johnny's phone. It rang four times, and his voice came through.

"Hey, Johnny Whoops here. Tell me something good."

"We found him! Billy's with me and Livie!" said Shirlee after the beep. "We're heading for the apartment." She pressed off and pocketed the phone.

At the same time, back on West Moore, Brick was shouting at the still groggy Manny.

"You goddamn cretin! How could you let that string bean of a kid get the drop on you?"

"I don't know, Brick. I was struggling with that broad who knew the kid. He came at me from behind."

"And you," Brick turned on Clifton. "Why didn't you tie him to the seat or something? Jesus, do I have to do everything around here? Plus he has my fuckin' car!"

"We'll get an Uber for Christ's sake. That thing's a rental anyway," said Clifton. "Think for a minute. There must be a reason his friend was here. This must be the place you've been lookin' for."

"Maybe," said Brick, talking a deep breath. "All right. Let's go." The three men walked back toward the office building. "Not you," indicating Manny. "We don't wanna scare 'em with a gorilla walking in."

Clifton and Manny exchanged glances. Manny stayed outside the building while Brick and Clifton entered. He'd had about enough of Brick's insults and bullshit but wasn't ready to leave his paycheck. Most of the work was easy. Usually simple intimidation of Brick's clientele trying to welsh on a bet. And driving his tall, skinny ass around town in a fine car. Before the Escalade, it was a Maserati sedan. Before that a Bugatti. Always a short-term rental and always expensive. Image was everything to Brick. This strong-arm stuff was new to Manny. Whenever things got dicey, Clifton was able to exert some simple physical pressure. People paid. Nobody wants a second broken arm after getting the first one cracked. But this? Brick kidnapping some kid? Hell, he'd seen enough cop shows to know that's a federal beef. Someone must be breathing hard down Brick's neck.

Inside Brick was making the acquaintance of Gloria in Dr. Marino's office. He laid on the smarmy charm.

"You sure don't belong in this crummy office," he said, a suggestive leer and raised eyebrows turning his face into a caricature of seduction. "If you worked for me, it'd be all play, know what I mean?"

"Do you have an appointment, sir?" asked Gloria, not appreciating the come-on.

"I'm sorry, Miss," interrupted Clifton, pushing Brick aside. "Pardon my friend here. He can't help himself when he sees an attractive woman."

Gloria sized up this guy. Much more her speed—tall, well built, sandy hair cut stylishly. Much better than this willow of a dude talking trash.

"What can I do for you?" she asked Clifton.

"A simple matter, really. Has this always been a dentists' office?"

That's curious, thought Gloria, looking at Clifton differently now. "Why do you ask?"

"Oh, we, er, we're location guys for a new movie. One of the scenes takes place in a dentist's office. You know, we're seeing if this might be the place."

"And what will I be doing for work while you make this movie?"

"You could be in the film," interjected Brick.

"All right now. Calm down, scout boy," said Gloria.

"Seriously," said Clifton. "You might be able to be an extra. We'd let ya hang around. Introduce you to a couple of influential friends." He laid on his sincerest expression.

"Well," said Gloria, thinking the line was doubtful. "That would be up to Dr. Marino. And the management company for the building. Servritt." She wrote the number down on paper with unicorns for the second time that day. "Say. Are you with the girl who came by earlier? She was very sweet."

"Yeah, sweet," said Brick sarcastically. He tore the unicorn note out of Gloria's hand.

"Come on," he said to Clifton, and they exited the building, finding Manny leaning against the wall. "So call Uber," he said to Clifton. He called.

CHAPTER 33

Billy drove the Escalade within a mile of Johnny's apartment, leaving it in an alley between two apartment buildings. Detectives Lapidus and Perry were standing in front of the apartment with Johnny when he, Olivia, and Shirlee approached.

Johnny spotted them coming and ran down the street to embrace his friend.

"Man, what the hell happened?" Johnny asked, out of earshot of the LAPD detectives.

"That asshole, Rick," said Billy. "Only his name be Brick. And he ain't no record guy."

"Ah," said Detective Lapidus, as the four approached. "Mr. Bates, glad to see you here. I wanted to speak to you as well as your friend here, Mr. Watson."

"Watson?" said Olivia. "Is that your name?" she asked Johnny.

"Johnny Whoops Watson, right?" said Billy, smiling at Johnny. "You can call me Billy," he said to Lapidus.

"Yes, all right, Mr. Bates," said Lapidus, taking a notepad from her pocket. "We went by your apartment earlier. We also spoke to Officers..." she checked her notes, "... Garcia and Rodriquez with Valley Division, the officers who responded when your place was burglarized." Billy nodded.

"They said nothing was missing? That's highly unusual for a burglary. No money gone, no jewelry. Nothing?"

"We don't have much," Olivia said.

"Yes," said Perry. "Ms. Feldon, correct?"

"Yes, 'correct,'" mocked Olivia. "You obviously already know that. Do you have any idea who killed my cousin Harry?"

Billy exchanged a quick glance with Johnny. The pieces were starting to fit.

"That's why we're here," said Lapidus. "Could we go inside?" she asked Johnny.

Perry, Lapidus, Olivia, Shirlee, and Billy followed Johnny inside. Billy pulled Johnny aside as they climbed the stairs.

"Johnny, that mofo was all crazed about me dad's old office. Maybe they thought Harry somehow knew where it was. 'Member? He was askin me bout it the night 'fore he died."

"Shit," exclaimed Johnny.

"Something, Mr. Watson?" asked Perry, who noticed the two boys talking. Johnny reflexively shook his head. "Mr. Bates," Perry continued, "...how'd you get that bruise on your forehead?"

"It be nothin," said Billy. "Fell off me bike."

They entered the apartment and crowded around the kitchen table, Olivia sitting with an audible sigh.

"As you know," began Lapidus, "...the late Mr. Feldon was a gambler. We have pictures here of some bookies who operate here in the Valley. We'd like you two, and in fact all of you, to see if you recognize any of them. Maybe you've seen Mr. Feldon talking with them. Take a look." She placed a pile of eight-by-ten photos on the table and fanned them out like a deck of cards, then separated one from the other.

They hovered over the photos. Johnny thought they looked like headshots he'd seen of actors. Except for the police line-up wall behind them all, measuring their height.

"There!" he said. "That guy." He was pointing to a picture of Brick, measuring six foot two. "That asshole claimed to own a record company and said he wanted to sign us."

"Yeah," chimed in Billy. "And we just got away from him and his goons."

"What do you mean, 'got away from them'?" asked Perry.

Billy told the detectives of being taken off the street, held in a garage somewhere, and transported to Moore Street. Olivia added details of her and Shirlee's journey to Moore Street, her discovery of Billy, and their escape.

"Their big Escalade is down the street," added Billy.

"Perry," said Lapidus. "Call in an APB on Bertrum 'Brick' Morgan Jr. He's not known for violence aside from some standard collections stuff. Maybe things got out of hand with Mr. Feldon."

"Or maybe Harry didn't give him what he wanted," said Johnny.

"Maybe," said Lapidus. "Let's inspect the car." She and Perry headed for the apartment door. "If you see him," she called back to Billy, "…call 911 right away. You might not be so lucky next time."

CHAPTER 34

Brick, Clifton, and Manny shared an uncomfortable and silent ride in a Toyota Corolla driven by a middle-aged Uber driver named Hartook, who enjoyed listening to the WAVE soft pop radio station. Hartook tried to engage them in conversation. Failing that, he sang along to Billy Joel and the Carpenters.

"Give me a good rating," he said as the three men exited the car at Hugo's, an upscale diner on Riverside Drive in North Hollywood. They ignored him.

Clifton and Manny went inside, Brick indicating he'd be with them in a minute. They took a table in a corner and ordered coffee. Outside, Brick dialed a number on his phone.

"Yes, sir," he said. "It's me. Yes. No. It's fixed; I got it." He gave him the address on Moore Street and the phone number of Servritt Management. "Yeah, it's an old office building with a dental office still there. Yeah. So the debt's clear, right? Yeah, sure, I understand. You'll see. It's the place. Yeah, OK." The line went dead. He looked at the phone for a moment and headed inside.

"Time to go," he said, taking a sip of coffee while standing by the table. "We should lay low. Head for Vegas 'til we know things are cool. Manny, get a car, and we'll meet here tomorrow morning, ten o'clock."

They split up, each in his own Uber.

Across town in Hollywood, a large, rotund man in a black Armani suit sat in a crimson Louis XIV chair. He commanded the room like a general on the battlefield or a captain at sea. Two other men were standing, waiting for orders. Both were over six foot, wore sharp suits, and had the rigid, alert bearing of men who'd been in the military.

"Wallace," the man said. "I want you to check the Board of Records. See if there's any historical documents linking this office building to Ted Bates. Price, you go to the building tonight. We'll see if our search has ended."

CHAPTER 35

Wallace dodged through three o'clock rush-hour traffic, weaving between cars and using the carpool lane, hoping to get downtown before the Hall of Records on Temple Street closed at five. With this lousy traffic, he thought, it won't be easy. It would have been easier to take the ridiculous Los Angeles subway. Who builds a subway system in an active earthquake zone? He imagined getting stuck underground in a seismic event. No way. Images of bombs exploding around him, dug into makeshift trenches in the dirt in Afghanistan flashed through his mind. He'd gone as a naïve nineteen-year-old and been back for ten years now, but certain memories never leave your mind.

He swerved around a platinum blonde in a pink Corvette who looked familiar as he passed the Capitol Records tower on his right. He thought he knew the blonde from somewhere but couldn't place her. Probably from some movie or TV show.

Six-five, salt and pepper hair cut tight to the scalp, two hundred thirty pounds, he sat ramrod straight but relaxed in the driver's seat, his eyes moving front to back, side to side, looking for an opening to scoot through like a running back looking for a hole in the defensive line. Drive to daylight. His cell phone rang. Wallace pressed the green button on the BMW M550i dashboard.

"Yeah, boss. In Hollywood still."

The husky, baritone voice came through the speaker in the car. "See if there's anything about this Servritt Management at the Hall. You might have to pay them a visit if Price can't find anything. They have an office in Echo Park."

"Right." The line went dead.

A building at 1722 Moore Street in downtown and Servritt Management in Echo Park. It had been and still was a predominantly Latino area for decades. Until recently when young professionals found it, realized the rents and home prices were substantially lower than on the west side, and moved in. The inevitable process of gentrification in a previously undiscovered section of the big city had begun.

He drove past Alvarado Street, the exit to Dodgers Stadium, and inched forward toward the skyscrapers in the distance. Another foolhardy idea. I hope they built those to advanced earthquake codes, he thought. Even so, he wouldn't want to be in one when a big one struck. The thought of swaying as if he was on a giant indoor wave machine gave him an instant of motion sickness. He breathed deeply, shook it off, and took the Temple Street exit, made a left, and parked in a lot on Spring Street, giving the attendant ten dollars. Wallace carried a leather attache case, looking like many of the other professionals, lawyers, accountants, and civil servants, walking into the adjacent courthouse, city hall, or other bastions of bureaucracy in Los Angeles. Wallace knew Parker Center, LAPD headquarters, was only a short walk north along with the city and county jails. He'd managed to avoid stays there and was determined to maintain that record.

He entered the imposing four-story granite building through heavy glass doors and asked the dark-haired woman behind the long marble counter for real estate records. He followed her instructions down the hall, up the stairs one flight, followed the hallway to the right, and entered a large library-like room. A young man wearing a white shirt and a red tie behind another counter pointed him toward the microfiche files containing records of real estate transactions and holdings prior to 2000. Wallace began his search.

At the same time, back in Hollywood, Lapidus and Perry were in the LAPD station parking lot, eating food truck burritos by their Ford Police Interceptor, a standard but specially equipped small SUV.

"These kids' story doesn't make any sense," said Perry, wiping chipotle sauce from his lips. "Why would a gambler like Brick need to know about this kid's dad's old office?"

"Maybe he's branching out, acquiring real estate," said Lapidus. "Or more likely, he's on an errand from someone else. Someone he's in hock to."

They decided to do their own research. They entered the squad room and sat at Perry's desk, calling up all known associates of Bertrum "Brick" Morgan Jr. on the computer. A list two pages long emerged, and Perry printed it out.

"Well, this'll take awhile," said Perry, handing the sheet to Lapidus.

"Let's get started," said Lapidus. They dissected the list for the rest of the afternoon, eliminating those who were dead or in custody, had left the state, or whose whereabouts were unknown. When the list was whittled down to twenty names, they found current addresses and headed back to their car.

CHAPTER 36

Johnny called Beans and Frank for a rehearsal the following night. It would get everyone's mind off the crazy events of the past few days and refocus them for their next job, playing back at Slim's next Saturday. He didn't want to disappoint Eddie, the club's owner/manager, who was always good for a gig, helping the band to maintain.

It was hard for Johnny to understand what had been happening. Was the break-in at Billy's not a junkie burglary and really related to Harry's death? There must be a tie there. Why else would that Rick/Brick character have scooped up Billy like that and driven him to this old office building? The girls, Olivia and Shirlee, were smart and daring to find and scope out the building like that, but they were lucky to have avoided Brick and even luckier to have found Billy. If Brick was there, he found that building, too. And now that he'd found it, maybe things could get back to normal. As if things are ever normal.

Like the Mark Twain quote—if you don't like the weather in New England, wait a minute. That's how he felt. For Johnny things were changing, slipping off in new directions faster than he could adjust. They were musicians and collectively were a band. Maybe this asshole Brick wasn't a record guy, but there were tons of others in this town. If

Philip M. Cohen

we keep on, keep playing, keep writing new songs, keep up club appearances, things will start to break. Even if most new artists these days record in their bedrooms with synth keyboards and drum machines. The pendulum's gotta swing back.

If only Harry was still around. He was always there with a positive word and encouragement, even when things looked bleakest. Now things looked bleak because he's not here. Some fool actually killed him. It was hard to fathom someone doing that to Harry. I just hope the cops get ahold of that Brick. That prick.

"Hey Billy," Johnny called out. Olivia and Billy had left the main area of the small apartment for the bathroom. That was an hour ago. Unless one of them was sick, they should have been done with their business by now. The bathroom door opened, and Billy grinned sheepishly, tugging on the rope holding up his pants. Olivia followed behind and scurried into the kitchen alcove where Shirlee was heating water for tea.

"Everything good?" asked Johnny, grinning.

"Oh yeah, mahn," replied Billy, lighting a joint. "It be jammin'." For a guy who'd had his place burglarized, a close friend killed, and been kidnapped, all in the last few days, Billy was remarkably resilient. Maybe it was all the weed he smoked. Or maybe he'd break down later.

"OK then," said Johnny. "Listen to this. I got a new song." He strummed an E minor chord and sang.

"What is the red, what is the white, what is the fear that keeps me up every night? / What is the shape of ghosts on the walls? Friends say it's nothing, but I see it all. / Lullaby, lullaby, with closed eyes I know who spies, / Lullaby, lullaby, all of the truth is all lies."

"Oh yes," said Billy. "You been internalizing, my friend. As all good artists do."

Olivia and Shirlee huddled close as Johnny played an instrumental bridge then sang another verse.

"Simply to nothing, nothing to clear, an image of dust, a phantom to fear, / A scream that I hear without any sound, a feeling of dread with smiles all around. / Lullaby, lullaby, with closed eyes I know who spies, / Lullaby, lullaby, all of your truth turns to lies."

"Yeah," murmured Shirlee. "That's it."

"Thanks baby."

CHAPTER 37

Wallace called from an alcove on Hill Street after spending hours researching files in the Hall of Records. Night had fallen, a dark blanket on the city, and a late November chill filled the air. Looking through those files was like being back in school, he thought. Only there were no sexy girls there to distract him. And he was a long way from Billings, Montana.

"Yeah? What'd you find?" came the baritone voice of the Boss on the other end of the phone.

"Not much," replied Wallace. He glanced around him, making sure no one was close enough to hear the conversation.

"How much, Wallace?" Irritation dripped from each syllable.

"No mention of a Ted or Theodore Bates relating to the property. It has been a medical office since it was built in '54, but there was no record of another dental office there before the present one with a Dr. Marino."

"And Servritt Management?"

"Listed as the property manager. Address is in Echo Park, 1709 Micheltorena."

"OK. Pay them a visit and find out what you can. Gently."

"Yes, sir. Of course." The Boss disconnected, and Wallace headed for his car. He cut into traffic on Hill Street, made a left onto Temple, a right on Broadway, and down the on-ramp to the freeway east toward Hollywood. It was the thick of rush hour, and he inched along for the three miles until the Alvarado Street exit. Making a left on Sunset, Wallace came to Micheltorena Street, a sharp right turn that ascended steeply up the hill off the boulevard. The address was half a block up, and Wallace parked on the dark street. A few people walked up and down the street, walking dogs, hurrying home after a long day at work.

The address was a single-story wooden home with a front porch and a sign over the worn wooden door proclaiming "Servritt Management." No lights were on inside. Wallace tapped on the door to confirm that everyone had left for the day, then casually walked around the house, searching for another entrance. The house was jammed into the hillside, and two concrete steps led to a back door. Wallace unsuccessfully tried the door knob, took out small tools, and jimmied the lock. With a penlight on, he was inside and stepped into a room that had been a kitchen but was now outfitted as a snack room—mini-refrigerator, microwave, paper plates, bowls, and cups in the cabinets. Through a small hallway was the main office. Two desks faced each other with matching office chairs on wheels. On the wall was a series of five file cabinets, marked "A-E," "F-J," "K-O," "P-T," and "U-Z." How very convenient, Wallace thought, as he popped open the "K-O" cabinet and rifled through the files, pulling out the Moore property documents. He quickly perused them, searching for some evidence of a Theodore Bates. Nothing. Servritt's records went all the way back to the '50s, but there was no mention of a Bates.

Wallace took photos of the paperwork with his cell

phone, closed the cabinet, and let himself out the backdoor. He had been in and out in ten minutes. He turned his car around on the narrow street, turned right on Sunset, and pressed a button on his phone.

"Talk to me."

"Nothing here," said Wallace. "If that guy had an office there, there's no record of it."

"All right." The line went dead.

At the same time, the Boss's other lieutenant, Price, was in Dr. Marino's dental office on Moore Street. Neither Gloria nor Dr. Marino were there, and Price had full access to the darkened space. But it wasn't files he was interested in. He went from room to room, tapping on the walls and testing the floorboards. Nothing in the reception area. Nothing in the first dental operating room. Price tapped on the blue walls of the second operating room, working his way around. Solid. Every tap was solid. He knelt and tapped on the white tile floor. Nothing…nothing…something. A hollow sound. He extracted his .44 from his shoulder holster, reversed it, and smashed the butt of the revolver onto the hollow sounding tile. It splintered. Price pulled the tile away and peered inside. Nothing. Just wooden beams, copper pipes and an empty space.

Price got off his knees, retraced his steps, and exited the building. Things were quiet on Moore Street. Thinning traffic passed, a car or two every couple of minutes. Price dialed the Boss.

"Price," the Boss's voice answered. "Tell me you found something more than Wallace did."

"Sorry, sir. There's nothing here. If Bates was here, he didn't leave anything behind."

"Damn!" A pause. "All right. We better have another conversation with Brick. And maybe that Rasta kid too."

CHAPTER 38

Brick was heading back to the restaurant parking lot to meet Clifton and Manny via Uber when his phone rang.

"Hey, that's my ringtone too," the Uber driver said.

Brick mumbled an obscenity as he fumbled the phone out of his jacket pocket.

"Yeah?" he answered impatiently.

"Brick." A statement, not a question. He knew that voice and was not happy to hear it.

"Yes, sir. It's me. Everything OK?"

"I'm afraid not. Where are you now? We should have a face-to-face."

"Well, I'm, er," Brick stammered, trying to think of what he should do. "I'm heading out of town. Next week?"

"Now, Brick."

"OK, can we meet at Hugo's in the Valley?"

"In an hour." The line went silent.

One hour. Manny and Clifton were meeting him in fifteen minutes. That gave him enough time to get prepared. Just in case.

Fifteen minutes later at the restaurant parking lot, Manny and Clifton were standing alongside a Chevrolet Suburban SUV big enough for a family of eight. Or four men Manny's size. Late-night diners were entering and leaving the parking lot—cars and SUVs carrying couples, young people in packs, single men eating alone. A late model Nissan Sentra pulled into the lot, stopped, and discharged a slinking Brick, waving his arms, motioning Manny and Clifton over. More trouble, thought Clifton.

"He's coming here," said Brick. "The Boss is meeting us here. That address was bogus, and he's not happy. We should get the hell out of here before he arrives. This your new ride?" he asked Manny, pointing to the Chevy.

"Hold on a minute," said Clifton, thinking it was interesting that Brick was saying "we," as if the trouble he was in was their trouble too. "If we rabbit, he'll be on us wherever we go."

"Yeah," said Manny. "You think he's not connected in Vegas? You'll be spotted the first day there."

"Yeah, yeah," agreed Brick, brushing strains of his thinning brown hair off his sweating forehead. "But we gotta be prepared. You guys wait in the shadows. He and his boys pull any crap, you'll have my back."

"Yeah, OK," said Clifton. Manny nodded his head in agreement. They walked to a dark corner of the parking lot, within sight lines of the front of the Suburban where Brick remained waiting, but hidden from view.

Brick spent the next ten minutes nervously pacing and checking the time. What does he want, he wondered. I gave him the building address. He checked his billfold. Five hundred dollars. Not even close to being enough to ease him off me. Damn.

Brick wasn't a gun guy. Made him even more nervous. That's why he had Clifton around. Plus Manny who spooked guys just standing there. But he had brought his snub-nosed

.22 with him, figuring he might need it in Vegas. Maybe he'd need it sooner than that. Like tonight. Can't have too much protection.

A white Maserati coupe turned off Riverside Drive into the parking lot and swung wide into a parking spot twenty feet from where Brick stood. Cars like this might have been unusual anywhere else, a few hundred thousand dollars of a machine pulling into a diner, but they were almost commonplace in Los Angeles. But the men exiting the vehicle weren't commonplace. Brick saw two tall, muscular, short-haired men, both wearing suits a little too small stretching over their taut physiques. One turned and opened the left passenger door. The Boss. As always wearing a dark Armani suit and looking like he was the lord of the parking lot, of the diner, the street, the valley, the entire city. An imperious look on his face as if he had stepped down from the heights to deal with the riffraff. And Brick was feeling exactly like riffraff.

"Brick," the Boss called. "Is that you over there? Come over here." He motioned him toward the Maserati. Brick hesitated, then approached him warily.

In the dark corner of the lot, Clifton cursed under his breath. Brick was leaving his field of vision. Clifton cautiously stepped out of the dark and into the shadows playing on the ground, leaving Manny behind, squatting besides the bushes lining the edge of the lot. Clifton pressed himself against the side of a black sedan, peeking over the roof.

"So, Brick," said the Boss, brushing some imaginary lint off his jacket collar. "That address wasn't any good. I wasted a lot of time and energy running it down, and you know what I got from it?"

"N…nothing?" said Brick.

"Right," said the Boss. "Nothing. So what am I to do? That address was in exchange for your debt. But you did not deliver the correct address. The debt is still outstanding." He turned to look in the direction of Price and Wallace, standing to either side of him. When he turned back, Brick had the .22 clutched in his fist and pointed at the Boss.

"Now this is disappointing," the Boss said. "Isn't this disappointing, boys?"

"Yes, sir," said Price. "Very disappointing."

Before the words were finished coming out of Price's mouth, Wallace took two quick steps toward Brick, levered his arm over Brick's arm, and pivoted the gun toward the ground. Wallace twisted, and the gun fell free, clattering on the ground. Wallace delivered a straight right into Brick's face, his nose shattering. Brick crumpled onto the pavement.

"I thought you had some smarts in that skinny little brain of yours," said the Boss, towering over Brick. "Now this is what you're going to do. You'll find out exactly where that Rasta kid is and let me know." He bent close to Brick's bloodied face and whispered. "One final chance. Do you understand?"

Brick nodded weakly. The Boss, Price, and Wallace left in the Maserati, leaving Brick on his knees. A young couple walked out of the restaurant, saw Brick, and quickly circled away from him. Clifton and Manny approached.

"You all right?" asked Clifton.

"Do I look all right?" blubbered Brick through the blood. Manny reached down, hooking Brick's arm to lift him off the ground. "Leave me alone!" He pushed Manny's arm away. "Where the hell were you guys? You're supposed to have my back. That's what I pay you for!" He pushed himself up and stood, wiping the blood from his face with his shirt sleeve.

"You shouldn't have pulled the gun," said Clifton. "What would you have liked us to do? Come in, guns blazing? Those two guys alongside the Boss would've cut us all down in seconds."

"Let's get out of here before someone calls the cops," said Manny. Brick let Manny guide him into the Suburban.

"We gotta find those kids again," said Brick. "Clifton, go by Billy's place again. And see if his band is playing somewhere. But we gotta do it soon. That guy's losing patience."

Clifton was too, but he didn't say anything. For now, he'd stick with Brick.

CHAPTER 33

Detective Lapidus sat at her desk in the Hollywood Station and stared into space. She was baffled; confused yet intrigued. All the pieces of this case fit like a jigsaw puzzle in her mind, but the pieces were slightly off, the edges rounded when they should have been sharp, or too big or too small to fit to the other pieces. She decided to use her old standby. Writing the elements of the case on paper and seeing if she could make them lock together.

They were:

1. The burglary at Billy Bates' apartment. The anomaly was that, as opposed to run of the mill burglaries, nothing was taken. Not that Bates had much of value except for an old TV. But if it was druggies, even twenty dollars for a TV was something, and it would have been gone. Whoever broke in there was looking for something but didn't take anything of notice.

2. The murder of Harry Felton. He was in hock to Brick Morgan, a small-time bookie and local thug wannabe. But that minor debt shouldn't have been enough for Morgan to kill Felton. Accord-

ing to Bates, a day before Felton was killed he was asking vehemently about Bates' father and an old office on a street named West Moore somewhere in L.A.

3. The kidnapping of Billy Bates by Morgan and the rescue of him on Moore Street near downtown. Another major crime, this one federal, resulting in an APB for Morgan. A familiar player like that shouldn't be so difficult to find and bring in, but for some reason he's been out of reach. He hasn't been at his usual place, the Yellow Dog bar in Van Nuys, and he's no longer living at his last known address.

Lapidus rubbed her temples and took a sip of the cold coffee in a paper cup on her desk. Perry had checked out the address on Moore Street after they had caught up with Bates and Watson two days ago. The receptionist there confirmed that, besides Olivia Felton, a man with a physical description matching Morgan had been there asking questions about the history of the office. Plus—

4. There was a burglary at the dental office on Moore Street the night after Bates' abduction and escape. Morgan again? Again, nothing was missing, but floor tiles had been broken. Whoever was there had been looking for something. But what?

The common denominator in all this is Bates. Billy Bates and possibly his father's old office. But what does a defunct dental office have to do with a small-time bookie? And what's so important about that place that someone would murder and kidnap to get it? What did Ted Bates leave behind?

Detective Perry leaned over Lapidus's desk and placed a cup of coffee down.

"At least it's hot," said Perry. "Probably not too fresh though."

"As usual," said Lapidus. "Thanks." She blew on it and took a sip. "Yeah, not too fresh. Any word on Morgan's whereabouts?"

"Nothing. He must be in the wind. No one with any brains would be hanging around after kidnapping and a possible murder."

"No one's ever accused Morgan of having an abundance of brains."

Perry snorted bemusedly.

"Let's pay Mr. Bates another visit," Lapidus said. "He's at the crux of all this. Maybe he knows more than he realizes." She rose, hesitated before leaving the coffee behind, swung her jacket off the back of the chair and walked out of the station, Perry trailing behind.

CHAPTER 40

Lapidus and Perry drove out of Hollywood on Cahuenga Boulevard, merging onto the 101 Freeway and heading into the San Fernando Valley. Reseda was near the center of the valley, northwest of Hollywood, a twenty minute ride when traffic was light, which was only at three in the morning—if there were no accidents. Now traffic was usual for L.A.—accordion-like. Cramped and stacked up for miles, cars eking along at 0–20 mph, then opening up for brief stretches, giving drivers a brief illusion of speed as they approached the 65 mph limit for a short distance, then back to the lineup, stacked and crowded like an In-N-Out drive-through at dinnertime or the parking lot at any Trader Joe's at any time of day. Lapidus was always tempted to flash the lights and zoom past all the commuters on the shoulder or the far left lane but, following policy, she knew that was for emergencies. Instead, she sped up and slowed down like everyone else on the freeway and the ride took forty-five minutes.

She parked across the street from the apartment house and noticed three men in front. One was tall and thin, one tall and muscular, one built like a brick wall. The thin one was pressing every entry button on the panel, obviously looking for a quick way in, a possible burglary. Lapidus and

Perry hurriedly exited their car to intercept them, when Lapidus put her hand out, stopping Perry in midstep.

"Wait," she said. "Isn't that Morgan?" She drew her standard issue .45. Perry did the same and followed Lapidus across the street. As the door buzzed ahead of them and Clifton pulled the door open, Lapidus yelled, "Stop right there! LAPD!"

Brick and Manny turned quickly and reached for their own guns. Clifton, already through the glass door into the apartment complex, sprinted inside the courtyard.

Perry yelled, "Guns!" He and Lapidus leaped behind a parked blue Chevy Silverado pickup.

Lapidus called out, "Drop your weapons! Morgan, we're bringing you in."

By the building, Brick yelled at Manny, "Cover me." He pushed Manny in front of him. Manny, in the open in front of the building, fired toward the cops, the bullets exploding into the pickup shielding the two detectives. From the left side of the Silverado, Perry edged out when the volley stopped, getting a view and fired two shots. Manny went down, sinking onto his knees, then folding in half, his chest and face slapping into the street.

From the right side of the pickup Lapidus sighted down on a running Morgan. One shot from fifty feet away and Brick cried out and toppled sideways, the gun clanging ahead of him off the sidewalk and onto the thin strip of lawn in front of the apartment building. Lapidus ran toward Morgan, Perry toward Manny, both with guns raised.

Perry kicked the gun out of Manny's hand, but Manny was never going to need it again. Perry's shots had hit him dead center, upper torso. He was gone before his face hit the ground.

"I'm going after the third man," Perry called to Lapidus, who was standing over Morgan. Blood was running from Brick's right thigh, where Lapidus's shot had struck and passed right through. Lapidus retrieved Morgan's gun, twisted his arms around, cuffed him, and called on her cell phone.

"This is Detective Lapidus. Shots fired. Requesting backup, ambulance, and coroner." She gave the address, switched off and looked at Morgan's puffed and blood-streaked face. "I didn't do that, Brick. Run into some tough characters?"

He answered by spitting blood and moaning.

Lapidus read him his Miranda rights.

"Don't bother. I've seen the TV cop shows," insisted Brick.

"All right," said Lapidus when she had finished. "Have you heard this? You're under arrest for the murder of Harry Felton and the kidnapping of Billy Bates."

Inside the apartment house courtyard, Perry held his .45 up and surveyed the courtyard and the surrounding second story. Nothing. He sprinted toward the stairs, bounding up two at a time. At the top, he paused, flattening himself against the wall and peering around the corner. Nothing. Perry ran past the string of apartments until he reached an emergency exit door. It was open. He rushed past it onto a landing above a series of stairs descending to a back alley. He ran down, but his quarry was long gone.

Perry rejoined Lapidus out front, two paramedics already lifting Morgan off the ground and onto a stretcher. They slid him into the waiting ambulance. Perry gave a description of the fleeing man to two of the half dozen uniformed LAPD officers who had responded to Lapidus's call, but it was too vague to be of much use.

Lapidus stopped the paramedics from shutting the ambulance doors on Morgan, a paramedic, and two uniformed officers before they drove off.

"Morgan, that goon of yours took off," she said. "Hope you weren't paying him much."

"Shit heel," moaned Brick.

"Who was he?" Lapidus asked. "He left you out in the cold."

"Fuck you. And fuck him too. Cut me a deal and I'll tell you all about it."

"Honor among thieves," said Perry as Lapidus slammed the door closed and the ambulance zoomed away, siren wailing.

CHAPTER 41

Later that night Billy and Johnny and the rest of Conflict were holding an acoustic rehearsal in Johnny's apartment, electric guitars and bass unplugged, Beans beating on a cajon—an oblong wooden acoustic drum originally from Peru but now popular with young bands performing non-electric music. With their next show at Slim's two days away, they needed to prepare.

"OK," said Johnny, after they had gone through a dozen songs. "So here's the set: 'Day of Days,' 'Till Yesterday Comes Again,' 'She Might Be Near,' 'Around the Bend,' 'Fifteen Secrets,' 'You Know It,' 'Let Me Go,' 'Crime and Banishment.' OK?"

Nods all around.

"OK then. Frank, Beans, see you Saturday at 7 at Slim's."

They packed their gear and headed out the door, brushing past Shirlee entering the apartment.

"You guys all done?" she asked, putting a plastic bag full of groceries on the counter. She began unloading, placing the eggs and milk in the refrigerator, the canned beans and a bag of rice in the cabinet.

"Yeah, Shirl," said Billy. "We be all good. Ya seen Livie?"

"Not since she left for school this afternoon," said Shirlee. "She should be back by ten."

"Right, right." Billy secured his guitar in its black hard case, retrieving a bag of weed from inside a compartment in the case. "Break time," he announced.

"I'll join ya," said Johnny.

"Me too," agreed Shirlee.

They stepped outside to a small balcony that overlooked the alleyway behind the building. Johnny leaned over the railing, spying down on his neighbors below. He and Shirlee often heard the couple in their early thirties arguing, usually about whether they were ready to have children. But all was quiet tonight. Shirlee joined him on the railing, curling into Johnny's chest.

"Hey, hey, lovebirds," said Billy, stepping out from the living/practice room. "If I may interrupt." He lifted a fat blunt, displaying his handiwork for all to see. He produced a Bic lighter from his pocket, snapped the flame on, and inhaled deeply.

"All right, Mr. Valley Rasta," a nickname Johnny had coined for Billy years before, "pass that thing over here." Billy smiled and handed the joint to Shirlee.

"Ladies first, mahn," Billy said. "And beauty 'fore age."

Shirlee took the joint, sucked in a small stream of smoke, and passed it to Johnny. He took a quick hit and let the joint dangle from the corner of his lips, doing his best Wild West outlaw impression.

"Da da da dum," Beethoven's famous opening played on Shirlee's phone in the apartment. She stepped back inside and answered it, asking, "Yes?"

"Ms. Shore? It's Detective Lapidus. Sorry to bother you this late, but I was hoping you, Mr. Watson, Ms. Felton and Mr. Bates could come to the station first thing tomorrow morning."

"Johnny has work in the morning starting at 11," Shirlee answered.

"How about at nine? Hollywood Station on Wilcox?"

Johnny stepped in from the balcony, eyebrows raised in a question. Shirlee soundlessly mouthed, "Detective Lapidus," and shrugged her shoulders. Johnny took the phone.

"Detective," he said. "This is Johnny. What's this all about?"

Lapidus explained that Brick had been apprehended earlier that night and that she and Perry now had some additional questions for them.

"All right," said Johnny. "If we can be done by 10:30, I can still get to work on time."

Lapidus thanked him and hung up.

"Looks like an early night," said Johnny.

The front door opened, and Olivia stepped in. She dumped her school books on the couch and flopped down next to them. Billy handed her the still-lit joint.

"When you gonna start wearing those sexy lawyer outfits?" he teased her. Olivia laughed and took a hit.

CHAPTER 42

Johnny drove his Civic early the next morning into Hollywood, Billy in the shotgun seat, Shirlee and Olivia in back. Rush hour traffic was bad, but it was only the usual logjam. He inched along, changing lanes occasionally, maneuvering toward the Cahuenga Boulevard exit.

Billy was all too familiar with the drive, staring out the side passenger window. In his first year after high school, choosing not to go to a four-year college and enrolling in two-year Los Angeles Valley College instead, he had gotten a part-time job at one of the many souvenir shops on Hollywood Boulevard that cater to the hordes of tourists who wander the boulevard year-round, especially during the holidays and spring breaks. The manager of the store, a kid named James, only a couple of years older than he was, thought Billy was overqualified, having actually graduated from high school and attending a college. But Billy liked the idea of being in the center of the action and convinced James to hire him.

He spent six months at the store, selling souvenir mugs and kitchen magnets with the word "HOLLYWOOD" emblazoned on them to families from the Midwest with star-struck parents and bored-to-tears kids, posters of female stars and L.A. beach beauties to Asian businessmen and barely pubescent boys, and pipes and cigarette papers to the score of kids strolling the boulevard on a weekend night. He remembered stepping out on the boulevard, watching the hookers bending into stopped cars, drug dealers leaning against buildings and whispering "pot, coke, meth" to passing potential customers, the costumed "actors"—Spiderman, Superman, Wonder Woman—making their way home after their stint in front of the Chinese theater, happy to come away with enough for rent for their badly furnished apartment in the Argyle Arms up the street. He felt comfortable and at home there.

Until that morning when Billy let in a street kid he knew as Rafe before opening. Rafe staggered in, high on poppers, and slammed into a glass display case, smashing it apart and slashing his own arm. Billy had tried to clean the damage, including the bleeding gash in Rafe's arm, but before he could finish James arrived unexpectedly. Seeing the glass damage, the blood drops on the floor, and the tossed and bloodied souvenirs, James fired Billy on the spot. His career as a boulevard salesman ended unceremoniously.

All this had occurred just two blocks from the Wilcox Avenue Los Angeles Police Station, in front of which Johnny now parked. He was wearing his security guard uniform as he had to head to Beverly Hills after meeting with Detective Lapidus, the others planning to Uber back. Johnny left his revolver in the glove compartment, knowing carrying a gun into a police station would be the last stupid move he would ever make.

The four friends climbed the concrete steps up to the station and went in. Behind a wooden counter high enough to intimidate anyone stepping up to it stood a middle-aged man in LAPD uniform, sergeant stripes on his sleeve. He loomed over Johnny.

Philip M. Cohen

"Help you?" the sergeant asked, looking dubiously at the four young people, especially at Johnny in his uniform.

"Yes," said Johnny. "We're here to see Detective Lapidus."

The sergeant shuffled papers in front of him, found what he was looking for, reviewed it, and said, "Right. Down the hall to your left, fourth desk on the right." He dismissed Johnny and the other three with a nod of his head in that direction.

Johnny led the procession down the hall. They passed a young Black man holding his arm and waiting on a bench along the wall, sitting next to an older Black woman shaking her head in disappointment.

"This is a little strange, doncha think?" said Billy in a hushed voice. "I don't like police stations." The memories of being picked up for vagrancy that time he cut school came to his mind, the threats by the cops, the hours spent waiting for his mother to show up, the thunderous lecture by his father.

"Just relax," said Olivia. "We didn't do anything wrong."

"Not this time, at least," said Shirlee.

They rounded the corner on the left and emerged into a large room, with green walls, full of desks stacked end to end. Officers in uniform and detectives in street clothes were standing and talking, drinking coffee, sitting and speaking on their phones, writing reports.

"Watson, Bates, over here," they heard from a spot fifteen feet to their right. Lapidus waved them over, standing beside a desk that was covered with paperwork. Perry was alongside her.

"Glad you could make it," said Lapidus, shaking their hands. Perry moved another two chairs up to the desk. "Everybody, take a seat." They arranged themselves around the desk.

"As I told you on the phone," Lapidus began, "Brick Morgan, the suspect in your kidnapping, Mr. Bates, was arrested last night. He was captured last night in front of your apartment, apparently looking for you again."

"But he got what he wanted," exclaimed Billy, turning heads of cops nearby. "He had the address on West Moore."

"That may be so," said Perry. "But obviously that wasn't enough."

"Right," continued Lapidus. "Now we've spoken to him. One of his men…" she checked some papers in a handheld notebook "…Manny Solango, was killed last night. The other escaped. Brick identified him as Clifton Case. This is a picture of him." She uncovered an eight-by-ten black-and-white photograph on the desk. "Do any of you recognize him?"

"He was on Moore Street outside the dentist's office," jumped in Olivia.

"And I think I saw him at Slim's last week," said Shirlee.

"Yeah," said Billy. "He was with Rick, er, Brick that night."

"OK," said Lapidus. "I don't think you'll see him again. We have the entire department looking for him now. But keep an eye out. They wanted that address bad enough to yank you off the street, Billy. We don't know why, but until we find Case, be careful."

"I've got to leave," said Johnny, standing to go.

"If you see Case," Lapidus said, "call me right away." She gave each of them another business card.

Billy, Shirlee, and Olivia stood to follow Johnny out.

"You're a band, right?" called Perry. "What type of music do you play?"

"They're a great rock band," said Shirlee, smiling broadly, ever the loyal supporter.

"Come out to see us," said Billy as they turned to leave. "Slim's tomorrow night."

Lapidus jotted a note in her pad as she and Perry watched them go.

"Whatever's going on," she said to Perry, "those four are in over their heads."

CHAPTER 43

Clifton took his shoes off and laid back on the motel bed. He was exhausted. Running was nothing for him once. In his Army days, running thirty miles, rucksack filled to fifty pounds on his back, that was routine. But that was also twenty years ago. He still kept himself in good shape, doing everything you'd expect a forty-five-year-old ex-grunt who prided himself on his youthful appearance to do. Jogging, weights, yoga, tae kwon do. Especially here in L.A., where if you don't keep up, you get left behind.

Still, running through alleyways and streets with busted-out lighting for over five miles, all the way from Reseda to this strip of hooker motels on Sepulveda Boulevard, took something out of him. Especially as he had to be wary of every cop he saw. Sweaty and looking guilty with a .45 tucked into his belt in the small of his back, he was an easy target for anyone on the lookout. And if Brick was still alive, he'd give him up in a blazing minute. That was a certainty. But he had reached safety for now. No one cared what anyone looked like in this dump. Most of the rooms were used for short-term stays, an hour or two, and the clerk downstairs didn't want or expect to see an I.D. or a credit card. Cash was king.

Philip M. Cohen

Clifton's eyes closed, and he began to drift to sleep. He rolled over onto his side, when a bulge in his pants pocket discomforted him. He reached down and pulled out his cell phone. Clifton opened his eyes and looked at it, then scrolled through the list of contacts. Unbeknownst to Brick, two days ago he had grabbed Brick's phone, scrolled to the Boss's number, and forwarded the closely held number to his own phone. You never know when it might come in handy. And now was prime time for it.

He pressed the number, and the line rang twice before a deep baritone voice said, "Who is this?" Pay dirt.

"This is Case," said Clifton. "Clifton Case. Former associate of Brick Morgan."

"Former?" asked the Boss. "Explain yourself and why are you calling me?"

Clifton explained his current circumstance and the possibility that Brick was either dead or in police custody.

"I see," said the baritone voice. "Well, good luck to you."

"Wait, wait," implored Clifton. "I can finish the job for you. For twenty grand I'll get the real address for you."

"Why should I trust you to be able to accomplish this task, Mr. Case? Your former employer was unable to do so, and you worked for him. Plus I have skilled employees of my own."

"I was hamstrung by Brick's incompetence and unjustified bravado. Look. Two days. Give me two days to get it. Ten grand." He needed at least that much to get far enough out of Los Angeles to be comfortable. Silence on the line for fifteen seconds. "Sir?"

"All right," the Boss said finally. "That address was a bust. And Servritt Management has no information about any Theodore Bates. That address you got was a waste of time.

But I'll give you one last chance. That White Rasta kid's band is playing a club on Lankershim in two nights. Like the entire naïve world, they put their business and personal whereabouts all over the internet. You'll find him there. Get me that information. You'll get your ten thousand." He ended the call.

All right, thought Clifton. A way out. He knew he'd be able to accomplish the task. One thing the Army taught him was how to be effective in extracting critical information from unwilling individuals. Especially when there were going to be so many of the kids' friends there.

Clifton stretched back out on the bed and shut his eyes. This will work out fine. Now if only that whore and john in the next room would stop moaning and banging on the paper thin walls of this dump.

CHAPTER 44

It wasn't so much of a dream. More of a waking illusion. A vivid picture of a world to be, a life yet to be lived, yet in the present, the here and now. With fevered colors, too bright, too alive, too shining. And smells that at once called forth scenes of childhood and made the hairs on your neck stand up. Like being at the edge of a cliff, the very pinnacle of the mountain and taking that final step forward into the abyss...and finding yourself asleep as your mother reads you a bedtime story.

Who could say it wasn't this way? Philosophers have tried explaining it in words, diagrams, and pictures for eons, but none have gotten it quite right. For they couldn't, you can't, I cannot. Words are puny things. Utterances that attempt to capture thoughts, impressions, feelings, longings, desires, acts. When those same thoughts, impressions, feelings, longings, desires, acts are only variations of the theme and not the theme itself.

Repeat after me...

Again...

So very good. All so wrong. The joy. The despair.

We're all going about this wrong. There is no wrong. We're doing the best we can. We'll all have to try a lot more. None of this matters. It's gravely important.

CHAPTER 45

Another night of rock and roll. Johnny and Frank, Billy
and Beans parked in the five-car parking lot behind
Slim's, the venue for tonight. They unpacked the equipment and set up again inside the club. It'd be their first gig
since they'd commemorated Harry's life at this same club
a couple of weeks ago. Johnny hoped people would show
up. A Thursday night in the Valley was a decent time for
a show, early weekend for some, but it wasn't a Friday or
Saturday. They put out the word as usual. A full-court press
by the four band members plus Shirlee and Olivia on Instagram and Twitter. They even went old school by posting
a notice on Facebook. Maybe some older guys from record
companies would see it there and show. Weirder stuff has
happened. Especially lately.

Johnny plugged in the cord from his Fender Strat into
the Ampeg amp on stage. At least he didn't need to bring an
amp. Slim's back line of drums, amps, and public address
system were set up, waiting for them to plug in and go.
Eddie stood at the control board of the PA, asking Billy and
Johnny to test the microphones for volume levels and tone.
"1, 2…" It sounded decent.

Beans tightened the heads of the drums, wanting to get
a higher tone, more attack. Frank brushed his long brown

hair out of his eyes, played a short run of notes on his bass and looked toward Johnny.

"OK," said Johnny. "Let's try one before people show."

"If they show," laughed Billy.

"Right. OK. 'Fifteen Secrets.' Ready?" Nods all around. "1, 2, 3, 4, 5, 6..." They swung into a looping groove in 6/8 time. Johnny played a short instrumental intro, and Billy sang.

"One, not something you should ever see/ Two, all the places where we could be/ Three, the triple threat that you abhor/ Four, the gentle kiss that I adore...."

"That's enough," said Johnny, halting the song in the middle of the first verse. "Let's not waste it."

Amid general grumbling, the band put their respective instruments down and huddled by a table at the side of the stage.

"How'd it sound?" Johnny asked Shirlee, hoping for a positive response.

"Oh, er, good, sounded good," answered Shirlee, distracted. "Did you see our new fans?" She pointed out a man and a woman standing by the bar. Lapidus and Perry. Johnny walked over.

"Hey," he said in greeting. "Didn't expect to see you here tonight."

"Yeah. We wanted to show our support," said Perry.

"Sure," said Lapidus, taking a sip of a carbonated drink.

"Need anything, Johnny?" asked Serge behind the bar, observing the cops talking to his friend. He didn't know why they were here, but he knew they were cops, uniformed or not, which usually meant no good in a music club. He'd seen too many people busted for minor nonsense like smoking a joint in the old days or even jaywalking in this town. Just cops looking to hassle kids.

Johnny caught Serge's vibe. "No, it's all good, Serge," he replied, reassuring the bartender. "Well, thanks for coming," he said to the detectives. "Enjoy the show."

"On in five," said Serge, wiping the bar with a white towel. "Rock this place."

Johnny saw that a crowd had formed around the bar, everyone getting a drink and loose for the show. People were lined up outside the front door, and Eddie was happily selling tickets for five dollars a head, 60 percent of which went to the band. Eddie took the other 40 percent, along with the much more lucrative bar proceeds.

"Lookin' large," said Billy, meeting Johnny at the lip of the stage. The crowd had surged past the bar onto the small chairs and tables nearby, onto the seats to the side of the stage, and finally crowding on the small dance floor.

"Johnny! Billy! We love you!" Johnny smiled at Shirlee's friend Charles, as always dressed to stand out, tonight in black and white polka dot pants and a fake brown fur vest covering his skinny bare chest.

Shirlee came up from behind, encircled Johnny, and squeezed. "Kill 'em, baby," she said, planting a wet kiss on Johnny's neck.

Johnny climbed on the stage. Beans was already banging out the rhythm to the first song on the drums. Frank came in on one in the next bar, laying out the descending bass pattern. Billy, standing next to Johnny at the front of the stage, played a contrasting lead line. The crowd started to move, all eyes in the club on the movement on the stage. Johnny stepped to the mic and started to sing.

"It's always something; always there/ The elephant in the room; the unbearable weekly fare/ The news makes me cry; the jokes just fall flat/ We've seen this show before; the situation's old hat…"

Johnny played a brief blues guitar line, filling the space between verses.

"But then there's you; glorious extreme/ Too young to stand alone; too old for memes/ Only you; always be there/ Standing like a queen; rainbow in your hair/ Always you…"

Billy echoed, "Always you."

"Always you"

"Always you."

Billy took the solo, bending the notes round and round, over and over, creating a whirlwind of notes, cascading into the lyrics that Johnny sang in the bridge.

"There's no time like the present; no, no time at all/ With you I'm in heaven; I run when you call…"

The band stopped. Then Johnny sang a capella, "Always you."

Billy echoed, "Always you."

"Always you."

The crowd echoed with Billy "Always you." "Always you." "Always you." "Always you." "Always you." Back and forth it rolled, between band and crowd, crowd and band, on and on, for what seemed like forever, until Frank played a sliding note on the bass, the entire band came in, and everyone—band and crowd—sang "Always you" four more times and Johnny brought his guitar down to end the song. The small but enthusiastic crowd roared.

They played for another forty minutes, one song after another, only losing the crowd when they attempted a cover of Weezer's "The World Has Turned and Left Me Here." The crowd was too young and the song too obscure. Or maybe they were already too drunk.

"Thank you all," said Johnny, the crowd cheering the last song of the set. "We'll be back in fifteen for another go-round." He placed his guitar onto a stand, jumped off stage, and put his arm around Shirlee. "Let's get high."

"I'm for it," said Billy, trailing them with Olivia into the parking lot. Frank and Beans followed, as did a short pretty brunette with long hair who had attached herself to Frank.

Johnny retrieved a large joint from his pocket, lit it, inhaled deeply, and passed it to Shirlee, who repeated the ritual. By the time it got to Billy for a second time, the joint was too small to hold. Billy tossed it on the ground and produced a second joint, lighting and passing it.

Johnny felt good. For the first time in weeks, things seemed right. The band sounded good, people were out supporting them, he and Billy were on the same wavelength, their girls were with them. Hell, they even had a couple of cops who might dig them. After everything that had happened, maybe the tide was turning. If they could play enough steady gigs, maybe he could even leave that security guard job. Although the training had been fun, the job itself was a dead bang bore.

"Hey, John," said Billy, breaking his pot-induced reverie. "I be thinkin'. Maybe my dad was more than a dentist. I don't really know what he was all 'bout 'fore I was born. Or when I was little. What if he was a drug kingpin? Or a mafia don?"

Johnny started to laugh. "Your dad?" He remembered Ted Bates as a small, thin, quiet, stern but unassuming man who never questioned his son's choices or made demands even when his only son picked up a guitar, decided not to go to a four year college, and braided his blond hair into dreadlocks. But he knew that Billy reacted differently to his father and had often described him as harsh and demanding. He could have been both, Johnny thought. "If he was, he shoulda been in the movies 'cause he was a great actor."

"Yeah, I guess so," agreed Billy.

"Hey, hey," yelled Eddie, sticking his head out of the back door. "You guys gonna play another set or spend the rest of the night getting high?"

"Do we have a choice?" joked Billy. He crushed out the joint on the concrete wall surrounding the lot, saving it for later, and joined his friends as they filed back inside the club.

The crowd had thinned. Even for young, hip denizens of L.A.'s nightlife, a work night was just that. After eleven, the first drinks are a faded memory, and the realization that tomorrow is another nine to five is gaining ascendance. Still, it was decent crowd for a Thursday night. The boys stepped onto the small stage, picking up their weapons of creative destruction. Johnny smiled at Billy, turned to Frank and Beans, and said, "Before and After." He sang:

"Before there was, was not time, was no space, was no was/ Before was, no one knows, just suppose, just suppose…" Billy played a single high piercing note for a count of three, and the rest of the band came in.

"A mighty light, a mighty roar, heavens soar, heavens soar/ Starlight borne, on a roar, silent roar, evermore…"

In the crowd on the tiny dance floor, Olivia and Shirlee were swaying to the slow, sweeping power ballad. Others in the crowd stared up at the band, broken from their conversations by the hypnotic sound.

"And after, oh after, after all, there is you/ After, oh after, you, you too."

Johnny launched into a solo, starting with single, distinct notes as the rhythm section of the band built a flowing wall of sound behind him. He built the solo step by step, note by note until the notes surged together in an avalanche of explosive power, culminating in a crescendo that shook the walls of the little club. The crowd roared its approval. Billy nodded at Johnny, who went into the next song.

Philip M. Cohen

CHAPTER 46

By one in the morning, the crowd had shrunk to a few hardy souls not wanting the night to end, not wanting to face a quiet or lonely and empty apartment, needing one last drink for fortification. Charles leaned against the bar, gazing into his drink as if the liquid had an answer for him. In the parking lot out back, Johnny finished stowing the gear. He banged the door of the Civic closed and asked Beans where Billy was. A shrug was Beans' answer, his usual hardly eloquent reply.

Johnny looked inside the club, spotting Charles at the bar, Serge putting glasses away, and Eddie counting out the receipts for the night at a corner table. Olivia emerged from nearby the stage, holding a bag of guitar cables.

"Billy asked me to grab these. He forgot them." She smiled ruefully at Billy's hazy forgetfulness. "Ready to go?"

"Where'd he go?" asked Johnny. "One minute he's putting his guitar away, next he's disappeared."

"You know Billy. He just stepped around the corner for a quick smoke." Johnny followed Olivia through the front door and around the corner. There was Billy talking to a guy several inches taller than him, wearing a UCLA Bruins baseball cap. As Johnny approached he saw the Bruins guy grab Billy by the upper arm and forcibly lead him down the street.

"Hey asshole! Let go!" cried Billy, his checkerboard Vans dragging on the pavement. Billy recognized him now. It was Brick's strong-arm man, Clifton, the same guy the cops had warned them about.

"Billy!" screamed Olivia. Johnny ran toward them, but stopped abruptly when Clifton, hand still gripping Billy's arm, turned toward Johnny and Olivia with a gun in his hand.

"Just stay calm, children," Clifton said ominously. "We don't want anybody hurt here, do we?"

Johnny stared at the gun. He flashed back on his training, but all they had told him for a situation like this was "if someone has a gun out, give him what he wants." But Johnny couldn't let Billy be dragged away for a second time in a week. He pushed Olivia aside and in a mad rush, screaming a battle cry at the top of his lungs, he charged at Clifton.

Clifton raised his gun toward Johnny, dead center, and pulled the trigger. At that same instant, Billy twisted out of Clifton's grip and slammed into his chest.

"Bam!" The bullet exploded out of the chamber, but went harmlessly into the air and to the right of an onrushing Johnny. He dove at Clifton's midsection, ramming into his stomach with his head and shoulders in an old Pop Warner football tackle, knocking Clifton to the pavement, Clifton's gun slipped from his grip, landing on the small patch of grass alongside the sidewalk by the street.

Olivia ran into the midst of the sprawling bodies, grabbed the gun, and shouted, "That's enough. Stop or I'll shoot."

Johnny and Billy rolled off Clifton, separating themselves from him by a couple of feet and out of the line of potential fire from the gun in Olivia's hand. From around the corner down the alley came Frank, Shirlee, and Beans, all stopping short upon seeing Olivia standing in a firing stance.

Clifton slowly pushed himself off the ground, one hand on the pavement, the other in the air.

"OK, OK," he said. "Take it easy with that gun. It's bigger than you are."

"It's not funny, asshole," yelled Billy. He ran to Olivia, reaching out to take the gun from her hands.

"Billy! Don't!" screamed Johnny.

As quick as a rattler striking, Clifton reached behind him, pulled a .32-caliber handgun from his waistband and brought it up to fire.

"Bam! Bam!" Two shots rang out in rapid succession, an instant apart. But instead of Billy or Olivia going down, Clifton spun to his left, his body thudding into the pavement, the gun flying from his hand.

From the shadows emerged Lapidus and Perry, their .45s still smoking in their hands. Perry shouldered his gun and ran to Clifton's prone body.

"Still alive," he announced. "One in the left shoulder, one upper left arm." Calling on his phone, he instructed the police switchboard operator to send an ambulance to the club's address.

Billy and Olivia huddled together, shock and adrenaline racing through their bodies, fighting for dominance. Shirlee and the rest of the band gathered around them. Lapidus approached.

"Everyone all right?" she asked. Nods all around.

"I didn't see you after the first set," said Johnny. "We thought you had left."

"Good thing you guys are a good band," said Lapidus, smiling. "Otherwise we might not have stayed." Seeing the confused look on Olivia's face, she continued. "Kidding. We knew there was a decent chance Case would show up tonight, so we stayed in the shadows most of the night."

Four LAPD officers arrived in two squad cars minutes before the ambulance pulled up. The paramedics attended to Case, wrapping his wounds for the ride to the police ward at the hospital. They placed him on a stretcher and loaded him in, one of the officers coming along.

"Maybe now we'll be able to piece together what's been going on here," said Perry, standing with Lapidus and the band and watching the ambulance drive off.

"We don't have it as fact yet," said Lapidus, "but Brick Morgan said Case was the one who shot your friend Felton. Why is another story."

Johnny and Shirlee, Billy and Olivia, Beans and Frank all retreated to the parking lot for the ride home after the tumultuous night. Perry and Lapidus drove off to the station to complete the never-ending paperwork. As they dispersed, two men sat in a black Toyota sedan parked across from the club, outside the shine of the street lights. The car pulled away from the curb.

"The Boss will want to know about this right away," said Price, hitting a preset on his phone. Wallace drove toward Hollywood.

CHAPTER 47

Two in the morning wasn't too late for the Boss, thought Wallace. He knew the Boss sometimes stayed awake for days at a time, while at other times he slept for twenty-four hours straight through. A normal eight-hour night was abnormal for him.

Wallace parked the rented Toyota on Selma, down the street from the office. Price got out of the passenger side, stretched, brusquely told the male hooker in tight shorts and a T-shirt who approached to take a hike, and then walked with Wallace around the corner. Hollywood Boulevard never completely shut down. The tourists might be gone for the moment, squirreled away in the hotels, motels, and day and weekly rentals on and off the Boulevard. But that's when the restless, hungry natives came out. Not having had their fill from the hours scavenging from the foreigners to Hollywood, domestic and not, they stayed out until their needs were satisfied. Or until the LAPD told them to move on.

They entered a building sandwiched between the Egyptian Theater, one of the oldest movie palaces in Hollywood and presently showing films from one of the town's "golden ages," and the Scientology headquarters. During the day young acolytes stand in front, egging on the tourists and lost souls to take their special Dianetics personality test. At this time of morning, however, all was quiet. Not enough souls to save, clear, and fleece. Wallace and Price climbed the stairs to the second floor. They tapped twice on the doorframe of number 207, no name on the yellow etched glass, and walked in at the sound of a buzzer.

The Boss was behind the desk. He might never leave that spot, thought Wallace.

"Come in," the Boss instructed, pointing to the two chairs in which they always sat, Wallace to the right, Price to the left. "Tell me everything you saw."

Price described their night, waiting in the car, watching as all manner of people wandered in and out of the club. "Like I said on the phone," said Price, "nothing went down until the end of the night. Then Case showed up and tried to drag the Bates kid off. But two LAPD detectives were there. They handled Case, who'll be recovering in the city hospital ward. We stayed out of sight per your instructions. Nobody knew we were there."

"If the cops were waiting for Case," said the Boss, "then they had to have decent information that he'd show up there. That punk Morgan probably gave him up. And if he'd do that to one of his own guys, he might make the mistake of mentioning my involvement in all this. And that would be very unfortunate."

Wallace wondered exactly what the Boss' involvement really was. There was a mysterious metal box lying somewhere in Los Angeles that the Boss was concerned about. But why was never made clear. And Wallace was too smart, too experienced to ask.

"Here's what we'll do," said the Boss. "Price, you keep a soft tail on the Bates kid. See if he pursues this business, looking for the address, searching old buildings. For all we know, that Moore address is completely useless."

"Right, boss," said Price.

"And you," said the Boss, pointing at Wallace. "Tomorrow morning I want you back at the Hall of Records. If this Ted Bates was in business in this town, which we know he was, hopefully there's records of it. Records that go back far enough. Got it?"

"Got it, boss," answered Wallace.

"All right, good night," the Boss dismissed them. They both rose, left the office, and joined the few souls still on the street.

The Boss remained at the desk, swiveling his chair around to look out the window at the relatively quiet street below. He'd been in Los Angeles forty years now. He remembered the old days when sex, drugs, and rock and roll dominated the city. He made his first fortune selling pot, then quaaludes, then coke in ever-greater quantities. First to kids on the Sunset Strip outside the clubs, the Whisky, the Roxy, Gazzarri's, the Rainbow Room. Then in ever-increasing quantities to the middle men who sprang up. Partying with Nick Casharian before the coke went to his head and he murdered those fools in the Canyon. Never to get out of prison.

And it was a simple matter to get into the sex trade. Back then kids, boys and girls, would come in off the Greyhound downtown every hour on the hour. A little friendly word, a place to sleep, some free weed or powder. Nothing to it. Before long he had a fine stable.

Those enterprises brought him into contact with all kinds. TV and movie stars, politicians, of course. Others who had their hands in various rackets. Entertainment magnates, real estate wheelers and dealers, construction tycoons who built this town. They say there's a fine line between the honest, hardworking businessmen and those who cut corners and take advantage of every opportunity that arises, right or wrong. To the Boss's mind, there was no fine line, no distinction at all. Everyone was out for theirs.

That's how he had met Ted Bates. Sure, he was a dentist. Nice, middle class, to all appearances a credit to the community. But he had secrets not even his family knew about.

1985. He had heard from a source that there was a dentist who was dealing pharmaceutical cocaine. The source vouched for him, and he met the dentist, who called himself Thomas Bishop but whom the Boss later learned was Ted Bates, at Musso and Frank's, only blocks from where he was currently sitting. A big neon sign out front proclaimed "Oldest Restaurant in Hollywood, 1919." It was a famous watering hole for celebs since the beginning. The Boss and Bishop/Bates had martinis, became friendly, and discussed the drug business and its potential.

After that, they went into business. Bishop/Bates was a solid drug source, and they had a fine working relationship throughout the white '80s, a time when cocaine was the drug of choice throughout the city, throughout the country. It had spread from the streets all the way to the boardroom. It wasn't only record company execs laying out lines for their artists and their secretaries and other underlings they wanted to fuck. In executive suites across the Fortune 500, CEOs kept the pedal to the metal, ingesting the powder as often as they would drink a cup of coffee.

The Boss found himself with all kinds of new opportunities. The Japanese construction boom of the '80s collapsed, and he was able to buy newly built offices and condos for pennies on the dollar. Secret casinos materialized in the shadow of the more legitimate poker palaces, where high rollers who didn't want to gamble in public played.

With money and connections came political influence. He controlled a majority of seats on the city council, directing favorable policy in zoning laws and permits.

Of course, the old standbys still operated. But instead of putting kids on the street, he furnished human product to his high-end clientele in first-class hotels and luxury suites. Coke was a steady earner, but so was Ecstasy, and now he had silent ownership interest in several "legal" pot businesses, both grow houses and your friendly neighborhood dispensaries.

Bates wasn't part of all of this. But he was involved in some of it until he became a father and insisted he had to get out of the life. He backed out, and the Boss, too busy with all his other action and with other drug sources readily available, let him go. But he always kept tabs on Bates and his family, as he did with all present and former business associates. He knew he had a son who had grown into a wacky kid with surfer blond hair tied into dreadlocks and dreams of making it as a musician.

All was fine, and he didn't worry about Bates until he heard a rumor recently that Bates had kept information on all the Boss's dealings stashed away. Maybe as insurance in case the Boss didn't like Bates leaving the business. But with the Boss working publicly with the mayor on a bid to build a massive housing project for the 2028 Olympics and to solve the city's housing shortage, he couldn't afford to let any old business find its way into the public eye. If he had only visited Bates in his old office.

Luckily, that asshole Brick Morgan had told him one of his marks was tight with a group of young musicians, one of whom had blond dreadlocks. And Price had confirmed it was young Bates. So everything was falling into place. As long as he got his hands on that secreted information.

CHAPTER 43

Another Thursday rolled around, and Billy was on his way to Woodland Hills for his weekly visit to his mother. Olivia sat next to him on the 750 MTA bus rolling down Ventura Boulevard. She looked especially pretty this morning, Billy thought, wearing simple jeans, pink T-shirt, and a short beige jacket. But the look on her face drew him in even more than usual. A calmness had enhanced her attractiveness, maybe due to the arrest of Brick and Case. Detectives Lapidus and Perry had reassured them that it was Morgan and Case, with the assistance of their driver, Manny Solango, who had planned the break-in at Billy's, his abduction, and possibly Harry's murder. Now they were in custody or, in Solango's case, dead. They all felt relieved, as if a major storm had passed and life could go on as normal. Johnny was back at his security guard job. Shirlee was still looking for work, but an offer to waitress at Art's Deli in Studio City was sounding pretty good to her. Olivia didn't have classes until later that afternoon. And Billy had the day off from Active, freed from standing around waiting for someone to come in and browse through T-shirts, jeans, and shoes.

Billy stared out the window and wished the bus didn't

have to stop seemingly on every block. He didn't want to get to the rest home too late. Not that his mother cared. She usually didn't know one in the afternoon from one in the morning.

Johnny had called him at Billy's apartment last night and hadn't been his usual cool "whoops"-like self on the phone. A guy who claimed to be a booker at the Teragram Ballroom on Seventh Street, near downtown, had called Johnny and asked about booking the band for a show in the near future. The Teragram was an old movie house in a not-so-great part of town that had been converted to a concert and dance hall. All kinds of musical acts played there, from current up-and-comers to established artists. And they swung from rock to pop, rap to reggaeton, salsa to country and western.

The music scene kept moving east—from the Whisky and Roxy on the Sunset Strip to Spaceland in Echo Park and now on to converted theaters like the Orpheum and the Belasco downtown and small clubs like Zebulon and the Lodge Room in Highland Park, northeast of the city center. It left a hole for music on the westside that clubs like Slim's and Maui Sugar Mill in the San Fernando Valley and old established clubs like the Troubadour in West Hollywood and the Mint in West L.A. sought to plug.

If Conflict could get into that scene, booking gigs at these new places, and brought along their usual fans and friends, they could really grow as a band. Maybe even be able to make a living off it, thought Billy. Chuck this sales job onto the side of the freeway.

"Billy," said Olivia, breaking his reverie. "Isn't this our stop? There's the IHOP across the street," pointing out their personal landmark.

"Yeah, right," he said, pressing the activator to signal the bus driver that a rider wanted off. Olivia exited down the steps in the middle of the bus with Billy following. They crossed the street after first checking for LAPD, who loved to give jaywalking tickets, primarily to young people, and entered the convalescent home.

"Hello, Billy," said Johanna, the woman at the front desk greeting him. He smiled back but didn't answer. Olivia thought he was being rude, but Billy never could recall her name. Even after visiting the place more times than he could count and the woman always there and always saying hello. He did know her name, just didn't remember it. Maybe it was the weed.

Olivia and Billy walked down the hall, passing rooms on the left and right. From some, the sound of daytime soap operas emanated, the overly dramatic music, the urgent tone of voice. From others drifted soft conversations, although Billy wasn't sure if they were all between two or more people or just one.

Billy expected to see his mother either looking blankly out the window or into space while sitting on her bed. So he was taken aback when he and Olivia stepped from the hallway into the room to see his mother sitting on the couch watching "The People's Court" on TV.

"Can you believe these people?" she asked rhetorically. "They are so funny." She laughed gleefully, tears rolling down her face.

"Hi, Mom," said Billy, not quite sure how to react. It had been weeks since his mother had been able to communicate with him, and he was no longer used to actually speaking with her.

"Hi, Mary," said Olivia, jumping into the breach. "How are you feeling today?"

"Oh Olivia, darling," said Mary. "I'm just fine, dear. It is so nice of you to visit. Did I ever tell you how much you look like my late husband's oldest sister? Barbara. Oh, she was a delight. And so pretty. Just like you." She smiled radiantly at Olivia.

"That is so sweet, Mary." Olivia came to the couch and sat next to Mary, holding her hand.

"Oh yes," continued Mary. "Why before you were born, William, the three of us—me, your father, and Barbara— would have so much fun together. Sometimes…" her eyes wide to Olivia, telling her a confidential secret, "…we'd stay up all night! Hah!"

Billy couldn't remember having ever met his Aunt Barbara. To him, she was a relative of the older generation who lived elsewhere and communicated twice a year with birthday and Christmas cards.

"Oh, we used to meet at the office on Westmoreland at the end of Ted's workday," Mary said. "And we'd go to Cassell's hamburger joint or the Pantry to eat, then maybe into Hollywood for a movie. Such fun. Oh, look at the judge," looking back at the television and giggling. "He's really laying the law down, isn't he?"

Westmoreland? Billy thought. Office on Westmoreland.

"Now Mrs. Bates, are you all right?" Ms. Lenore, the attendant entered the room. She saw Mary's face, bright and alert. "How are you, Billy? Isn't this wonderful, how your mother is?"

"Yes, yes," said Billy, distracted by his own thoughts now. "Yes, it's great."

"Who are you?" asked Mary, suddenly fearful and not recognizing Ms. Lenore. "What are these strangers doing in my room? Why is the TV on?" She sank into the couch, covering her face with her hands.

"Now, now, Mrs. Bates," assured Ms. Lenore. "That's OK. You know me. Let me help you back into bed."

"No!" Mary vehemently responded. "Get away. Barbara will help me, won't you, Barbara?" She looked questioningly at Olivia.

"Yes, of course, Mary." Olivia took her by the hand, leading her off the couch and tucking her into the bed under the blanket. Ms. Lenore shut the television off.

"OK, Mom," said Billy. "You rest, and I'll be back soon." He bent to kiss her on the forehead. Mary didn't move.

They left the room in silence, Ms. Lenore accompanying Billy and Olivia to the front lobby and exit.

"It's sometimes like that," said Ms. Lenore in sympathetic explanation. "One minute she's fine, the next she's somewhere else. Such a shame. Well, we'll see you next week."

"Did you hear that?" Billy asked Olivia as they walked up Ventura Boulevard toward the bus stop.

"Hear what?"

"Westmoreland. Not West Moore. Or Moore Street. Westmoreland. That's where my dad had his old office. Whatever it was Brick and those guys were looking for, they were in the wrong place. We gotta tell Johnny."

"But what was it, do ya think? Why go to such drastic lengths?"

"I don't know. But we gotta check it out. What if there's a hidden treasure chest?"

"Oh, Billy. I'm sure. Full of doubloons, I bet." She laughed. "Don't be so dramatic." She squeezed his arm.

They stood together on the corner, watching traffic, searching for the bus. Across the street, in the IHOP parking lot, Price watched the couple as they stepped onto the bus and headed east on the boulevard.

CHAPTER 43

While Billy and Olivia were visiting Mary, Wallace was spending another day at the Hall of Records. This time, however, he was checking on businesses, specifically dental offices in Los Angeles from the 1980s. Every business in the city (at least every legal one) had to obtain a license to operate, all for a fee paid to the city comptroller. Wallace hunkered down with microfiche files and a reader, going through the vast collection.

Thankfully, the categories, if not the actual records, had been computerized. Wallace browsed through all medical categories first, isolating the dental records. Armed with this information, he was able to isolate those records, pulling the microfiche only for dental offices. Still it was an all-day job as there were dozens of files to scour.

Wallace went through the files on the screen, searching alphabetically. Unfortunately, the *B* as in Bates did not come up in the first few files. The *M*'s were before the *N*'s but after the *Q*'s; the *H*'s were before the *I*'s but after the *L*'s. This scattershot method of looking for a simple file, which with modern technology should have taken minutes, was taking all morning. At some point, Wallace thought, they'd have to computerize all this for simplicity's sake. But either due to manpower shortage, funding difficulties or both, he still had to use 1980s technology for a twenty-first century problem.

After more than two frustrating hours of searching, Wallace stood and realized he was hungry. His favorite burrito stand, Los Burritos, was a short drive back toward Hollywood on Vermont Avenue, a few blocks north of Los Angeles City College. Price had introduced him to this little joint when he first arrived in town. A machaca burrito sounded really good about now.

Wallace left the Hall, pulled his car out of the nearby parking lot, and, eschewing the freeway packed with midday commuters, took Temple Street west. He followed the street out of downtown, through Echo Park, and made the slight left where the street changed to Beverly Boulevard. Stopped at the light at the next intersection, Wallace looked at the street sign above. "Westmoreland." A bell went off in his head. "Westmoreland!" Not "West Moore." Everything made sense to him now. All thoughts of food left him. He made a screeching U-turn, stomped on the gas pedal and raced back to the Hall of Records.

By the time Billy and Olivia made it back to their apartment, night had fallen. Outside Price watched and waited in his car, mindful that Bates might never come up with anything, but aware that if he and Wallace fell down on their respective assignments, the Boss had been known to display his unhappiness in very unpleasant ways. And even for a professional like Price, he'd prefer to avoid such confrontations.

Price's phone rang, its ringtone like an old-fashioned corded tabletop model. It was the man himself.

"Yeah, Boss," answered Price.

"Where are you now?" the Boss asked, wasting no time with pleasantries.

"Outside the kid's apartment. He visited an old age home in Woodland Hills earlier, and now he and his girlfriend are here."

"OK. Come back here. You're done for the night."

"You sure?"

"Just come back. Wallace scored the info we've been searching for." The Boss hung up.

Price started the car and headed toward Hollywood.

CHAPTER 50

"I'm tellin ya," insisted Billy. "I'm sure of it. Westmoreland. We gotta go there and find that place."

Johnny had been listening for over an hour to Billy expounding on the great revelation he had speaking with his mother, Mary, while she was coherent, how this was the key to everything that had happened the past few weeks, and that they were going to discover his dad's secret mystery. He couldn't recall Billy ever going on like this, talking a mile a minute and not stopping for breath. Excited wasn't the term for it. He was supercharged.

"Billy, man," Johnny said. "Chill down, brother. You know it's been almost thirty years since your dad worked there, even if that is the right place. Anything he left behind is probably long gone."

Shirlee walked by, carrying a bottle of Corona and giving Johnny a knowing shake of her head. She sat on the couch next to him and pressed the remote, flickering the TV screen on.

"Hey, look," she exclaimed, pointing at the screen. On the TV, Detective Lapidus was identified in letters under a video of her talking to a Channel 4 reporter.

"Detective Lapidus," said the young reporter with long blond hair, "we understand you have a statement to make to the general public." She put the microphone under Lapidus's mouth.

"Er, yes, that's correct," replied Lapidus, looking into the camera and, although Billy knew it wasn't so, seemingly directly at him. "We have captured the individuals who committed a series of crimes in the San Fernando Valley in the past week. However, we still do not have a clear motive. If anyone has further information on these crimes, including a murder in Studio City, please contact the number below." A phone number displayed below her on-screen. "Thank you."

"I should call her," said Billy. "She should know about Westmoreland." He reached for the phone and dialed.

"Wait a minute, man," said Johnny. "Maybe we should check it out before letting the cops chase their tails around."

"Johnny's right," said Shirlee. "This is just a hunch you have. And even if it's right, we have no idea how it all fits."

"All right then. Let's go," Billy said, hanging up the phone. He slipped on his jacket and headed for the door.

"Now? I've got work in the morning," complained Johnny.

"Yeah, now," insisted Billy. "Either you come along or give me the keys."

"OK, OK, I'm coming." Johnny lifted off the couch and headed for the door.

"Don't forget me," insisted Shirlee. "Whaddya think, Livie?"

"Not me. Go have fun chasing phantoms in the dark." Olivia switched channels, getting comfortable on the couch.

"OK, later," said Billy as he, Johnny, and Shirlee left the apartment and headed downstairs to the beat-up Civic. They piled in and drove east toward downtown Los Angeles.

Hearing the car motoring down the street, Olivia dialed a number on her phone.

"Hello, LAPD?" she asked. "I have some information."

Philip M. Cohen

CHAPTER 51

Midnight on a Wednesday is a fine hour for commuting in L.A. In fact, it's that brief window when you can actually utilize the normally overcrowded freeways in the manner for which they were designed—being able to get from one end of town to the other easily, quickly, and without much hassle. And that might have been so in the 1970s. Now you have to hit that window. Unless it's raining. Or there's an accident. Then it's business as usual. And something was causing the backup tonight.

Johnny sat behind the wheel on the 101 Freeway, staring at the line of cars ahead, to his sides, and behind him. The Capitol Records building stood alongside the freeway, a stack of concrete vinyl playing no hits tonight. The car radio was tuned to KCSN, the Cal State Northridge radio station, which was playing unknown songs by unknown local bands.

"We should be on this station," said Billy. "Our stuff is as good as this."

"Our stuff can be as good as Jack White's," said Johnny. "But until we get it recorded, no one will ever hear it on the radio."

"Will you guys stop arguing?" said Shirlee. "Can't we get out of this traffic? Johnny, use the streets."

Johnny pulled off the freeway at Gower and went east on Hollywood Boulevard. They may not make better time because of the traffic lights, but at least they had the illusion of movement. They passed the neighborhood known as Thai Town east of Western and continued toward Vermont Avenue, passing the old sign for the now-defunct Hollywood Billiards on the corner. The boulevard cut diagonally into Sunset Boulevard and continued east toward downtown.

"Where precisely are we gonna look, Billy?" asked Johnny. "Google Maps shows Westmoreland stretches in sections from up near Sunset to way south."

"I don't know. But I'll know it when I see it," he replied.

"OK," joked Shirlee. "E.S.B. Extra sensory Billy."

"Make a right here." Billy pointed out the window. There it was—Westmoreland. Johnny turned the car, and they drove past worn single-family homes with ragged front lawns and concrete front steps with cracked and faded paint. On the same block were three-story apartment buildings left over from the fifties building boom. Dim streetlights shone down on a string of cars ten years and older lining the curb. The same scene repeated for close to a mile until the street ended. Johnny turned right, then left on Vermont for a half mile, and circled back to where Westmoreland continued.

This was more of a commercial strip. There were old homes, but these were interspersed with commercial buildings, old but some still in business. Bodegas, Thai massage parlors, tax preparation and insurance offices. Many of the business were in buildings that looked as if they were homes at one time.

Johnny drove slower now, the three of them craning their necks out the window, trying to see anything that would indicate a current or former dental office. Suddenly the small car rocked as a Toyota sedan came zooming down the street, doing sixty, passing the Civic as if it were parked.

"They're in a hurry," said Shirlee indignantly. "They could kill someone driving like that."

"Hey, wasn't that car parked outside the club the other night?" asked Johnny. He pressed down on the gas pedal and followed the path of the Toyota.

"Whoa!" cried Shirlee. "Johnny, slow down! There's a million cars like that in Los Angeles." The car rocked back and forth, bumping along the potholed streets as Johnny tried to catch up to the car ahead of them.

"No, that car was outside the club the other night." Johnny passed Wilshire, approached Olympic, and spotted the car idling outside an abandoned building marked for demolition. A sign overhead advertised a future mixed-use development—retail and commercial—that would occupy the entire block.

Two men exited the Toyota and walked toward the building. Johnny drove past the men and turned the next corner, quickly stopping and turning off the car. He reached into the glove compartment and pulled out his work revolver, sticking it into his waistband.

"Johnny!" cried Shirlee in alarm.

"You stay here," he told her. "This isn't fun and games anymore. You too, Billy."

"But…" Billy protested.

"No way, man," said Johnny. He quietly closed the car door and walked around the corner, staying close to the buildings. The streetlights were out in this forsaken area, providing Johnny with the cover of darkness.

"This is the address," said Wallace. He and Price exited the Toyota and walked up to the chain-link fence surrounding the building and future work area. Wallace snapped the lock on the fence with a tire iron from the trunk. The lock clattered to the ground, and Price pushed the fence open wide enough for them to pass through. They covered the fifty feet from the fence to the building in seconds.

Up the steps to a door leading into the two-story building. Price nodded at Wallace to bust the door knob, but when Wallace tested it, the door swung open. They stepped through.

Behind them, Johnny was watching their movements and stealthily approached the fence. If they find anything, they'll be coming out with it, thought Johnny. He decided to wait outside rather than confront two guys who were more than likely armed and surely professionals. He knew they were involved somehow with everything that had been happening.

Inside Price found an old building directory laying on the dirt-strewn floor. An Issac Shapiro, DDS, was listed in suite 205.

"That's the suite listed for Theodore Bates at the Hall," said Wallace.

Two elevator doors were on the opposite wall, but their operating condition was suspect. Wallace found a door to the stairs, and they climbed to the second floor. The closed-in stairs were dusty and smelled of mildew and garbage. The door to the second floor was jammed. Wallace kicked it open with his steel-toed shoes, the door crumbling off its hinges into the hallway.

Price and Wallace stepped over the fallen door and found 205 on the right side. This time Wallace found the door locked shut. He pulled out the tire iron and slammed it down on the doorknob. It splintered off, and they stepped into a waiting room that no human had been in for years. A ripped orange plastic couch sat against one wall in front of a cracked glass coffee table. On it lay copies of Car and Driver, People, and Sports Illustrated magazines from 2015. Opposite was a reception desk behind a sliding yellowed plastic window. Alongside the reception desk was a door to the offices. Price and Wallace pushed through and began to search.

Outside Johnny waited with a view of the front of the building. Time dragged. He checked his watch. 2:30. There was no telling how long those two would be in there. He was thinking of going back to the car when he heard, "Johnny. Johnny." He nearly jumped into the air. Billy.

"Billy, get out of here. Don't leave Shirlee alone in the car," he admonished.

"No," Billy said. "She sent me out here to check on you. You OK? Mahn, it's awful dark out here."

"That's a good thing. Well, since you're out here, I'll check on Shirlee. You keep an eye out for those two." Johnny handed Billy his Glock. "You remember how to use this?" Johnny had taken Billy to the firing range in Burbank after Johnny became certified as a security guard. "Remember, keep the safety on unless there's real trouble. I'll be back in a minute." Johnny went off into the darkness toward the car.

Billy looked at the gun in his hand and shook it, feeling its weight. He lifted it in a shooting stance and mouthed "pow" like a kid playing cops and robbers. He posed like James Bond, gun pointed muzzle up and to the side of his face, and looked around with what he imagined were steel-gray eyes, hardened by a thousand adventures. A noise by the building stopped his playacting. The front door of the building was opening, and the two men were stepping down the steps. One of them was carrying a small case.

Billy looked around for Johnny, but he was nowhere to be found in the dark night. The two men were close to the chain-link fence, only a few dozen feet from the shadows of the building where Billy pressed himself against the wall.

All Billy could think was that they were getting away. And they had his father's secrets in their hands. He stepped out of the shadows, pointing the gun at the two men, and yelled, "Stop!"

Surprised, Price and Wallace wheeled around to see Billy standing there, gun upraised. They could see his arm shaking. Like the trained professionals they were, they inched apart, creating two targets.

"Don't move!" Billy yelled. "Drop the box."

"Take it easy, kid," said Price. He bent to lower the case onto the ground, then sprang back up, reaching into his shoulder holster. A shot rang out, and a bullet kicked up dirt by Price's feet.

"Drop your weapons," commanded a woman's voice from the other side of the fence. "LAPD."

Lapidus and Perry stepped out of the shadows, guns out. Price lifted his left hand in the air and slowly moved his right hand off his shoulder holster. He feinted surrender, only to drop to a knee and fire. Lapidus and Perry hit the ground at the first movement, laying prone, their guns pointed in Price's direction. Return fire blasted, and Price went down.

Billy stood in shock through the exchange, too surprised to react. But Wallace wasn't. He had raised his hands at the first order from Lapidus, but as soon as Price fired, he took off, running for the street and the Toyota. Perry fired in his direction, but the lack of streetlights hindered his aim. Bullets ricocheted off the sidewalk and against the parked cars. Wallace reached the Toyota, jerked open the driver's door and began to launch himself inside, only to be tackled, a body hitting his midsection with a jarring crunch. He slammed against the open car door and onto the ground, a thin, wiry body on top of him.

Johnny furiously punched down onto Wallace's upturned face. A loud crack, Wallace yelped, and his nose was fractured. Blood spurted over Wallace's face and onto Johnny's hands. Wallace whipped his face left and right, clearing his vision and heaved his large body upwards. Johnny flew backwards, bouncing against the chain-link fence. Wallace scrambled for the open car door, but before he could get fully in his feet were grabbed. Johnny held on despite Wallace's frantic kicking. One foot got loose, and Wallace pushed Johnny in the jaw, too close to effectively kick him. Johnny tumbled away from the car. Wallace fumbled for the ignition, started the car, put it in drive, and he was gone! he thought—until he felt cold steel pressed against his temple.

"Freeze, asshole," hissed Perry, standing alongside the Toyota. Wallace took his hands off the wheel and raised them in the air. Perry, the .45 still on Wallace, reached in and turned off the ignition. He grabbed Wallace by the shirt collar and dragged him out of the car, cuffing him while Wallace was on his knees.

"Nice tackle, kid," said Perry to Johnny, who regained his feet. "You're pretty tough for a rock 'n' roller." Johnny laughed. Billy ran up to him, the gun waving in the air.

"Hey, hey," Perry and Johnny yelled simultaneously.

"Man, give me that thing," said Johnny, taking the gun from Billy. "Since when are you a gun-wielding badass?"

"Since now, mahn," grinned Billy.

"Johnny, are you OK?" Shirlee came running once the sounds of gunfire had stopped. Johnny held her in his arms, reassuring her.

Perry shoved Wallace toward the Ford sedan around the corner and locked him in the back seat. He joined Lapidus, who was reading Price his Miranda rights. A bandage was wrapped around Price's upper left thigh where the bullet had struck.

"Nice shot, Detective," said Billy as he, Johnny, and Shirlee joined them.

"Thanks," said both Lapidus and Perry. They looked at each other, grinning.

"We'll let the crime scene boys figure it out," said Lapidus. "They're on the way." As she said this, two squad cars pulled up, along with an ambulance and another unmarked detective car.

CHAPTER 52

J ohnny, Billy, and Shirlee stayed at the scene of Price's shooting until the early morning. Lapidus then let them go home and get some sleep after telling them to come to the Hollywood Station to answer more questions later that afternoon.

Billy wanted to go to the Original Pantry on Figueroa for breakfast, but Shirlee and Johnny were too spent, too exhausted to eat. They headed back to Van Nuys, where Olivia, who also hadn't slept, opened the door to the apartment. They all collapsed and didn't wake until early afternoon.

Johnny called into work, telling them he had a bad cold. Going into full detail was both unnecessary and far too complicated.

A couple of hours later, the four friends were huddled around Lapidus's desk in the Hollywood Station, styrofoam coffee cups in their hands. Billy explained how his mother had, in a moment of lucidity, mentioned the street name "Westmoreland," leading them to spend the previous night hunting for a dental office thirty-years defunct. Johnny jumped in, telling Lapidus and Perry about the black Toyota sedan barreling down the street at midnight and how he recognized it from the other night, the first night that

Lapidus had come to their rescue. But there was one thing that puzzled him.

"How did you know where we'd be?" asked Johnny.

"You can thank Ms. Feldon here," replied Perry, indicating Olivia. "She called last night. We cruised Westmoreland and finally saw your car parked. It was only minutes later that the fireworks started."

"Thank goodness," said Olivia.

"Then why were those guys last night so anxious to find this old dental office?" said Lapidus. "Morgan and Case either didn't know or wouldn't give it up, and Wallace and Price, the two from last night, are both claiming they don't know."

"Did you find the box?" asked Billy.

"This?" asked Perry. He placed the case that Wallace had been carrying out of the old building on the desk. It was aluminum, gray, eight inches wide, ten inches long, and three inches deep. "Since it was first taken from an abandoned building and is now evidence, we took the liberty of opening it."

"What'd ya find?" asked Billy excitedly. He stood and hovered over the box.

"Nothing," said Lapidus. "At least nothing to connect it to murder, kidnapping, and general mayhem."

"It does have your father's name in it though," added Perry. He opened the case and stepped back, allowing Billy to look.

Billy peered in. Paperwork was lined up in partitioned sections, each section beginning with a heading. At the front of the case, the words "Dr. Theodore Bates" were typed on a piece of deteriorated cardboard.

Billy flipped through the case. He extracted a piece of

Philip M. Cohen

paper from the first section. "Peter Aramis" was listed at the top, followed by dates and dental procedures. "9/16/85 2nd left molar, filling." Billy picked out another. "Sally Wilson" "2/5/87 root canal."

"What is this?" cried Billy, exasperated. He pulled out more and more paperwork, each with the same type of information.

"Looks to me like simple dental records," replied Lapidus. "We'll go through it, and we have people searching the building now. But unless we find something unusual, there's nothing to go on here. Everything in this case appears to be old, run-of-the-mill office records."

The air seemed to go out of the room. After so much anticipation and so much drama, it all amounted to nothing, thought Billy.

"Come on, Billy," said Johnny. "Let's go home."

"We'll let you know if we find anything," offered Lapidus, as Johnny, Billy, Shirlee, and Olivia filed out of the station. It was a typical sunny day in Los Angeles, warm and not a cloud in the sky. But gloom pervaded the mood of the four friends.

Johnny drove the Civic north, passing Hollywood Boulevard, up into the Cahuenga Pass, and northwest on the freeway. Nobody spoke. The radio played the newest hit by Drake featuring Rihanna. Johnny felt dislocated and tired. Billy was simply confused.

CHAPTER 53

A week had passed since his men, Price and Wallace, had been picked up by the police. If they had only surrendered immediately, thought the Boss, the cops would have booked them for simple trespassing, perhaps burglary for that useless box they found, and they would have been released within hours. As it was, Price had to play cowboy and shoot it out with the police. Now they were both being held for aggravated assault and attempted murder, plus trespassing and burglary.

It was a good thing they had only known what to look for but not why it was so important. And being good soldiers, they would keep their mouths shut.

Two detectives, a woman named Lapidus and a Black guy named Perry, had come to see him two days before. They had hunted down connections between Price and Wallace and him, and had tried to pry information out of him. Of course, he said nothing, letting his lawyer, Cy Friedman, do his talking for him. The cops came away with zero.

So maybe that's all it amounted to. Nothing. Maybe it was just a rumor that Ted Bates had perpetrated in order to keep him neutralized from acting against the skinny weasel. If the cops had found something, Friedman's spies in the D.A.'s office would have gotten wind of it by now.

The Boss sighed in relief, looked out the window at Hollywood Boulevard, and imagined moving downtown to his new mega-complex in a couple of years. Life went on. And life was good.

———

Life went on for Johnny and Billy as well. The mysteries surrounding them weren't resolved, but they had no time to dwell on it. Johnny went back to his work at the office building, Billy at the shop. Shirlee took a waitressing job at the new and improved Norm's Restaurant opening on Ventura, and Olivia kept working to complete her paralegal degree. Frank, turning all of eighteen, ran through another half dozen girlfriends before graduating high school. Meanwhile, Beans had taken a gig with a touring band and was on the road.

Even so, things continued to progress for the band as well. Not that Conflict was touring or playing Zebulon, the new hip place in Highland Park. They still had yet to record their tunes or get anything up on YouTube or SoundCloud or even build much of a presence on Instagram. But the possibility of playing the Teragram Ballroom was still dangling out there. And in the meantime, Rog, the manager of the Whisky, had called and offered them a gig opening for the old San Francisco punk band the Dead Kennedys. With no ticket sale guarantee! To Johnny, he could almost imagine that he was going to be living back in the old Hollywood days. The days of the Byrds, the Doors, Buffalo Springfield, or Van Halen, X, Devo, all playing the Sunset Strip to the overflowing crowd of young hippies or the next generation, the punks.

Olivia, who had always loved the band's songs, convinced first Billy and then Johnny that she was the perfect replacement for Beans, even if the only music lessons she had ever taken were on piano. But that, she assured them, was more than many famous musicians had ever done. Since they did not expect Beans to be back in time for the gig, and there was no timely alternative, they agreed. She bought a used set of Roland electronic drums and could be heard pat-pat-pattering away every minute of her spare time in the apartment she shared with Billy. Billy invested in a pair of noise-canceling headphones.

CHAPTER 54

A few days later Billy and Olivia took the bus to Woodland Hills to visit his mother. Ms. Lenore, who Billy felt always cared about his mother more than he'd expect most nursing home employees to, had called and said Mary had been asking for him and wondering where he was. Her dementia seemed to be accelerating and, even when lucid, she was more and more agitated. According to Ms. Lenore, Mary was alternately calling for Billy and for Ted, Billy's father.

Billy anxiously looked out the window of the MTA bus, nervously tapping his foot on the floor. Olivia covered his hand with hers in Billy's lap.

"My playing is really getting better," she said, trying to distract Billy from his thoughts about his mother. "I know I'll be ready by next week." She had progressed to playing along to roughly recorded versions of the band's songs.

Billy half smiled, his lips tight. The stress of the last few weeks was bearable, but the ill health of his mother was a burden too much. He felt like running away. But where was there to go?

"Come on, Billy. This is our stop." Olivia stood and, leading Billy by the hand, stepped off the bus. They crossed the street and entered the facility. Johanna, the receptionist behind the desk, nodded a greeting to them as they passed, walking toward the corridor leading to Mary's room.

"Mary, Mary, come down from there." Billy heard Ms. Lenore's voice as they turned the corner leading to his mother's room. Mary was standing on a chair, reaching up to a top shelf of the closet in her room. Ms. Lenore was standing alongside, imploring her to get off the chair, her hands steadying the chair.

"Mom, what are you doing?" Billy asked, rushing to her.

"Boxes. It's all in boxes," said Mary, pointing to cardboard boxes on the shelf that she couldn't reach.

"Let me help you. I can reach it." Billy helped her off the chair and took her place, stretching to grab the three boxes and handing them down to Olivia. As Olivia placed them on the floor, Mary opened the boxes and threw their contents all over the room.

"Ms. Bates," said Ms. Lenore. "What are you doing?"

"Ted. Ted," cried Mary, strewing the paper all around her.

"Mom, what is it?" asked Billy, bending to look through the mess at a piece of paper. He stared at the yellowed sheet. "What is this? I've never seen these." There were photos of his mother and father from before he was born, standing in front of a building that looked familiar. A sign on the street read "Westmoreland Ave." "Hey. This is the building from last week." He showed it to Olivia.

"They must have taken it when your dad had his office there."

"Oh, we had the greatest fun," said Mary, her eyes turning bright. "Partying with Bobby Jackson and his friends all night long. You kids didn't invent drugs and rock and roll, you know."

"Mom!" exclaimed Billy. He picked up another piece of paper. "Wait a minute…"

"What, Billy?" asked Olivia. She reached for a piece. There was a date, "11/14/89, R. Jackson, $50K to Councilman Flores." She read out loud the next. "12/10/91, R. Jackson, 20K to Assemblyman Siegel."

Billy shuffled through the paper. "1/15/90, R. Jackson, 10K to Supervisor Richmond," he read. "This must be it! This is what Brick and all those other assholes were looking for the whole time."

"You have to call Detective Lapidus," said Olivia. She began piling the papers back into the shoeboxes. Billy climbed back on the chair and pulled down another two boxes. Inside were more slips of paper with similar jottings. He dialed a number on his phone. It rang three times, and a female voice answered.

"Mr. Bates," said Lapidus. "How can I help you?"

"I think I can help you, Detective." Billy told her what he had found.

"R. Jackson?" said Lapidus, thinking out loud. "Isn't Robert Jackson the head of RJ Building and Construction? Give me the address of the nursing home. I'll be there in a half hour." Billy recited the address and hung up. A huge grin spread across his face.

"See?" said Olivia. "You never know what will happen."

CHAPTER 55

A week later, Johnny and Billy stood outside the Whisky on the Sunset Strip, looking up at the sign over the corner of the club. "The Dead Kennedys" on top, "Conflict" below.

"Second time playing the place, and we're on the billboard," said Johnny proudly.

"And in second position," agreed Billy.

"Out of two acts." They laughed.

It was 8:00 p.m. The band had arrived at the club two hours ago, loaded their gear in, set up, had a sound check, and gotten high. All necessary prerequisites to truly enjoying the night. Set time was 9:00. Olivia stepped into the night from inside the front entrance to the club.

"This is so exciting!" she said, wrapping her arms around herself, trying to contain the electricity pulsing through her body.

Billy grinned at her. "Ya li'l rocka you."

"Just remember the stop at the top of the bridge on 'Never, No,'" said Johnny, referencing their opening song.

"Yeah, I got it," she said. "I taped a copy of the set list on the bass drum." Johnny, Billy, and Frank had their own lists taped to their amps.

"How does the set play?" asked Billy.

"Seems fine to me." Olivia had graduated to playing on acoustic drums at a rehearsal space in North Hollywood and then rented a set for this gig from the Guitar Center in Hollywood. Turns out she was a natural behind the kit.

"Johnny, Billy!" Charles, wearing black and white polka dot pants and a maroon shirt, bounded around Larrabee Street and embraced both boys in an awkward hug. "This is great. The Dead Kennedys, Jello Biafra. He's a legend."

"Glad you could make it, bro," said Johnny. I guess Shirlee's social media efforts for this gig had some impact, thought Johnny.

Charles talked with Olivia and Billy, gossiping about people they knew, those who had gotten in trouble lately, either with friends, family, or the cops, and those who had mysteriously had a run of good fortune—not that usual here in Hollywood.

Johnny checked his watch. Still some time before they had to get on stage. The line outside the club was building, extending up the sloping street, an even mix of older, longtime fans of the headlining band and younger people curious to see the famous/infamous act. Graying longhairs stood alongside kids with shaved sides and high coifs of multiple shades, pink, purple, and black. Jeans and t-shirts, the uniform of the people, were still the order of the day for most.

One couple stood out in the line. A middle-aged White woman and younger tall Black man. Johnny poked Billy and pointed to the couple.

"Look who's here," he said. Walking up the block, Johnny and Billy greeted Lapidus and Perry.

"Detectives, here undercover?" joked Johnny. He had never seen them except in suits. Now Perry was in jeans,

Lapidus in slacks and a colorful serape. They blended right into the multihued crowd.

They hugged and clasped hands.

"We had to see our favorite young rockers and amateur detectives," said Lapidus.

"Nice turnout," said Perry.

"Oh, they're not here for us, really," said Billy.

"Well, we are," said Lapidus.

"You're the media stars," said Johnny. "We saw you the other night on the news making the arrest announcement." He recalled watching the local newscast in fascination, along with Billy, Olivia, and Shirlee, as Detectives Lapidus and Perry stood at a lectern outside city hall, announcing that they had made a major arrest in a fraud, bribery, and racketeering case that extended back decades against Robert Jackson of RJ Building and Construction. Someone had tipped off the media on the arrest that morning as the live press conference was interspersed with video of Robert Jackson, known to many in the city as the Boss, a coat ineffectively covering his face, being led out of a building on Hollywood Boulevard, rushing past a young man on the street holding a Dianetics book and a young woman in maximum makeup and minimum clothing, and being inelegantly shoved into a squad car. According to Lapidus, further indictments were expected for various former and present city, county, and state officials following additional ongoing investigations. A city councilman had then taken the microphone to announce that all present and potential contracts with RJ Building and Construction were being suspended pending the results of the investigations and any trials.

"Come on, guys," said Shirlee, rushing up to them. She was decked out in a silver miniskirt, white flowing blouse, and white platform shoes. "Rog is getting heated. He wants you on stage in five minutes."

"That's fifteen minutes in rock time," said Billy.

"See you in there," said Johnny to Lapidus and Perry. "Enjoy the show."

"Break a leg," called Perry. "Do they still say that?" he asked Lapidus.

CHAPTER 56

Johnny surveyed the crowd surging below him in waves from one end of the room to the other. The lights had been dimmed to almost dark, but he could see faces in the crowd. There was Lapidus and Perry, standing against the first-floor bar that curved around the open space dance floor/mosh pit in front of the stage. There was Charles, jumping up and down in the front row of the balcony, unmindful of the drink sloshing out of the glass in his hand. There was Rog standing next to the soundman at the board in the corner of the floor, holding up one finger to indicate time left before they were to begin. And there was Shirlee, a beautiful beaming vision, looking up at him from the lip of the stage, happy and thrilled to be here at this moment in time with the people and the man she loved. And he loved her too.

"2, 3, 4…" Olivia called out, then a crack, and the band launched into the song. Johnny sang:

> *"Tell me, why's it have to be this way,*
> *Why me, more than any other day,*
> *Hear me, honey let me say those words,*
> *Tell me, why's it have to be this way.*
> *You can't find anything underground,*

    Philip M. Cohen

I can't listen to a single sound,
All of our friends are falling apart,
There ain't no cure for a broken heart..."

Billy tore into a stinging guitar solo, flailing his blond dreadlocks in front of his face. Johnny pumped out the chords and looked back at Olivia, who was pounding away at the drums, born to bash. Frank stood in one spot at the corner of the stage, his fingers moving up and down the fret of his bass guitar, too cool for school, a coven of young girls standing below, staring up at him.

"Now you're everything that I need,
"Everything that I need,
Everything,
That,
I,
Need..."

CHAPTER 57

A single note contains the immensity of every moment. A single tone embodies all images, thoughts, creations, worlds. There is no time, no present, no future, no past. Only this. This is everything and all. This is why we are, who we are, what we are. The single beat of the heart encompassing every beat that ever was. Let this moment last.

Philip M. Cohen

Made in the USA
Las Vegas, NV
24 January 2024

84827959R00121